"Here." Cooper [...] have a look."

He held his arm out, and when she approached, he put his arm around her shoulders and tugged her close to him as if he'd been doing it for years. He pointed up to the sky.

There, dancing in the heavens, were the most beautiful, celestial lights she'd ever seen. Greens, reds, golds. The colors of Christmas.

"It's the aurora borealis," he explained, his arm still around her shoulders as if it belonged there.

It felt so nice she had to resist the urge to snuggle into him. Wrap her arms around his waist. Which was just plain wrong considering she'd vowed to not even *think* about a man, let alone cuddle up to one, until she got herself back to the Audrey she respected.

A moment's weakness, she told herself. She'd just poured her heart out to him. That, and she was drawn to him. A man who understood what it felt like to love and lose, then wonder how on earth to get up again.

Dear Reader,

There are times when I sit at my desk and dream up a story to tell, and times when one hits me in the face. In this case, it was definitely the latter. Last Christmas, we arrived in Scotland to find my father-in-law very ill in bed. He was refusing to go to the hospital but clearly needed help. We called his local GP. Within an hour, a doctor was by his bedside to help. Two hours later, two district nurses arrived, also to help. Throughout the entire Christmas holiday, including Christmas day, they came and gave him the medical care we were unable to, and continued to care for him after we had to get back to the animals at our farm. I was humbled and impressed by the level of care and compassion they showed, and vowed to tell a story that showed just how large an impact these health workers have on the people they care for. As ever, please do feel free to get in touch!

xox *Annie O'*

CHRISTMAS UNDER THE NORTHERN LIGHTS

———

ANNIE O'NEIL

HARLEQUIN

MEDICAL
ROMANCE

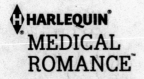

HARLEQUIN®
MEDICAL
ROMANCE™

Recycling programs
for this product may
not exist in your area.

ISBN-13: 978-1-335-14981-7

Christmas Under the Northern Lights

Harlequin Enterprises ULC
22 Adelaide St. West, 40th Floor
Toronto, Ontario M5H 4E3, Canada
www.Harlequin.com

Printed in U.S.A.

Annie O'Neil spent most of her childhood with her leg draped over the family rocking chair and a book in her hand. Novels, baking and writing too much teenage angst poetry ate up most of her youth. Now Annie splits her time between corralling her husband into helping her with their cows, baking, reading, barrel racing (not really!) and spending some very happy hours at her computer, writing.

Visit the Author Profile page
at Harlequin.com for more titles.

This book is dedicated to Scarlet Wilson, a fellow writer and a wonderfully dedicated district nurse who worked throughout the COVID-19 pandemic with her usual flair and panache. You, and the countless other nurses like you, keep the world a better place. Thank you.

CHAPTER ONE

AUDREY LEANT AGAINST the ferry railing to peer into the cloudlike sea mist. If she spread her arms out wide she'd look just like the heroine in *Titanic*. Excepting, of course, the tiny little differences.

She was a short-haired brunette, not a ringleted redhead. She was wearing woolly tights and about nine other layers of clothes versus an opulent gown and a neckline dripping in jewels. Plus, she was nowhere near being able to afford a maid or first-class passage to Scotland, let alone America and, more to the point, she was completely alone. No Leo in sight.

Sigh.

Not that she wanted one. Too rakishly handsome. Too much potential for her to be snared and then, without so much as a moment's notice, dropped like a hot potato. At Christmas. Well. The lead-up to it, anyway.

Her thumb skidded along the smooth terrain

of her ring finger. Yup. Still empty. That was what happened when you threw your diamond ring at your naked fiancé and his…whatever she was. Elf? Santa's little helper? Super-svelte Mrs Claus?

It had been hard to tell, seeing as the curvy blonde had grabbed all of her Christmas-coloured clothing and clutched it to her *entirely naked* body as Audrey had absorbed the fact that someone who wasn't her was having sex with the man she was meant to marry on Christmas Eve.

Time, it turned out, did stand still sometimes. And not really when you wanted it to. She'd always remember the look on Rafael's face: sorry, but…not sorry.

His lack of contrition had ripped open her deepest, darkest fears and laid them bare. He'd not really loved her at all. Hadn't meant a single one of the sweet nothings he'd whispered, nor a single, solitary promise that he'd made. She'd thought he'd been the answer to all her hopes and dreams, but it had all been a mirage. Seeing him look at her without a fraction of remorse… She'd never felt so small.

The only good thing to come out of the roiling mess of emotional debris was the vow she'd made. She would never, *ever*, let herself be led up the Swanee ever again. She was mistress of her own destiny from here on out. New job. New home. New life. For the next five weeks anyway. Even if it all felt absolutely terrifying.

Fighting the inevitable sting of the tears that had been lurking, un-spilt, these past three days, she spread her arms out wide, relishing the assault of wintry sea air.

'Eh, lassie! You'll not want to fall into those murky waters.'

Audrey lurched in surprise, nearly doing precisely that.

The man, a member of the ferry crew if his uniform was anything to go by, grabbed hold of her until she was steady again. She threw him a semi-grateful smile and then her eyes flicked up. *Ugh.* Perched atop his knitted blue cap was a headband bearing two multi-coloured, fairy-lit reindeer antlers.

She grimaced. Couldn't he see she was having a *moment*? A melodramatic moment, to be sure, but it was certainly a step in a better direction than drowning in a sea of her own tears— the more likely option if she'd stayed in London. Stupid London, with all its cheery Christmas lights and decorated windows and restaurants and bars bursting with yuletide cheer and mistletoe kisses. And, of course, her ex-fiancé. She was well shot of the place.

'Consider me duly warned,' she said, in a tone

that sounded miles away from the Audrey she used to be.

What a difference seventy-two hours and a bit of awkwardly placed tinsel could make.

The sailor gave her a *your call* look and took a step back. 'Fair enough. Advance warning, though. When we hit the dock there'll be an almighty thud. You'd be best to come back away from the railings.'

As if actual bruises would be a problem. He should see her bruised heart. 'And how long will that be, then?'

He squinted into the murk, then gave a nod as if his X-ray vision had just clicked in. 'About ten minutes. Twelve, max.'

Plenty of time to get her Kate Winslet vibe back.

She gave him the side-eye, which proved sufficiently powerful to get him to back off.

Alone again, she closed her eyes and shook her head, willing the bracing North Sea wind to blow the dark memories away. When she opened them again everything looked just the same.

Miserable.

It was only two o'clock in the afternoon. It got dark *early* up here in Scotland. If she hadn't triple-checked the boat's destination a dozen times before and after boarding, Audrey might easily been convinced they were heading to a wintry Brigadoon rather than her new island posting: the Isle of Bourtree.

The town was called Bourtree Castle, which had sounded promising in the same way Windsor Castle did, but a quick internet search had made it pretty clear Bourtree Castle was no place for royals. Tiny population. Ever diminishing. The 'castle' was actually a pile of rocks. And the only way to get to Bourtree was by the ferry. Which only ran three times a week.

Trust her to find the one locum position in a Scottish Bermuda Triangle. Perfect for the way things were going for her. Very, very badly.

She let go of the railings again.

'You're not the locum district nurse, are ye?'

Audrey whipped round. This guy had most certainly never seen *Titanic* and— Wait a minute… 'How did you know?'

The twenty-something redhead shrugged, his felt antlers bobbing in the wind. 'I know everyone else on the boat, and Coop said I should keep an eye out for you. So…*voilà!*' He spread his hands out wide. 'Job done. Welcome to Bourtree.'

He nodded out towards the foggy gloaming beyond the boat where, now, she could just see the odd twinkle of light.

'And Happy Christmas.'

Bah! Audrey scowled. *Christmas.*

She replayed everything he'd said. 'Hang on a minute. Who's Coop?' There'd been no mention of a Coop when she'd got her posting.

'Dr MacAskill.'

She was still none the wiser. 'And he is…?'

'House calls doctor. Well, he's a flash A&E doc from Glasgow, but he's come back to Bourtree to help out until they find a proper replacement for Old Doc Anstruther. He's retiring.'

'Ah.'

It was an awful lot of ancillary information. If memory served, she was pretty sure Dr Anstruther was the one she was meant to contact regarding her accommodation. With her luck it'd be a leaky igloo.

'Folk want him to stay on, but no one's banking on it.'

'Who?'

The sailor shot her a *keep up* look. 'Coop.'

'Oh?'

'Yeah. He's island born and bred, but…' He stopped himself mid-flow, as if he were about to give away a state secret. 'Anyway, they're taking bets down the Puffin, if you want to lay down a fiver.'

'What's the Puffin?'

'Pub. It's where pretty much all social life

begins and ends on the island. You'll find out all you need to know about Cooper and anyone else on the island if you sit there long enough. So mind you don't do anything too outrageous, because before you know it all of Bourtree will, too.'

Intriguing. And also annoying. If he was doing house calls that most likely meant they'd be teamed up when necessary. She really could've done with working on her own, using the downtime between patients to sort the rest of her life out. Then again, this 'Coop' character sounded a bit of an enigma. Focusing on someone else's dilemma would be better than thinking about her problems.

'Why wouldn't he stay? It's a nice place, right?'

Please, please, please say yes.

'Ach, it's nice enough. But Coop's not lived here for fifteen years. For what it's worth, I think he'll stay. It's not like back in the day when—' Another guilty look pulled him up short.

'Understood,' she said, not really understanding at all—but what did it matter? She was leaving in five weeks. If this Coop character left tomorrow or stayed forever it wouldn't matter a hill of beans to her.

More importantly, it was growing increasingly tricky having this conversation with the sailor. His nose was bright red with the cold, and looking him in the eye was virtually impossible with the blinking antlers bobbing in and out of her eyeline.

She drudged a bit of civility from the caverns of 'The Audrey She Used To Be', gave him a polite smile and said, 'Happy Christmas to you…erm…'

'Scottie,' the man said, with a light touch to his knitted cap.

He turned and went, the sound of a whistled 'Silent Night' travelling in his wake.

Bleurgh.

Christmas.

Even so…just because she wasn't getting married in three weeks' time didn't mean *everything* was awful. She had a five-week locum post that would allow her to recapture the passion of her true calling: district nursing. And the accommodation that came with the job would keep her off the streets until she figured out what to do next. She had several hundred miles of cushioning between her and the wedding she'd no longer be having.

What a fool she'd been to pay for the celebration herself. She'd thought it would act as proof that she wasn't marrying Rafael for his money. Or his movie star good looks. Or his charm. A triumvirate of desirables that he clearly felt free to spread around.

Fat lot of good the wedding insurance had done her. They didn't pay up when you cancelled because your fiancé was a snake.

C'mon, Audrey. He's an out-of-the-picture snake now. It's your life. Your destiny.

As she plumbed her brain for another nugget of positivity, the cosy faux fur lining of her coat nestled against her neck. There! She was warm. She gave the puffy down ankle-length coat a grateful pat. It had been her final purchase before leaving London behind…perhaps for ever. Pristine white, able to withstand arctic cold and, as an added bonus, two deep, hand-warming pockets. A winter essential up here in the North Sea—even if it had reduced her bank account balance to zero.

But now that Christmas was off, she was newly homeless, and was going to have to start her whole entire life over again, thanks to her lying, cheating ratbag of an ex-fiancé, a little bit of comfort shopping had seemed necessary.

Her phone buzzed deep in her pocket.

She pulled it out. A message from a number she didn't recognise.

Dr MacAskill here. AKA Coop. Hope you're ready to hit the ground running. Several house calls to make when you land.

This, followed by a slew of Christmas emojis.

Oh, good grief. This locum posting was beginning to hit a rather unpleasant chord. An 'out of the frying pan into the fire' type of chord.

At least there was work to do. If she couldn't spread any cheer, the least she could do was help improve people's health. Seeing patients had a way of reminding her just how fragile the lives everyone led could be.

She'd learnt that particular life lesson the hard way. Her mum had passed away when she'd been a little girl and her father, after devoting himself to raising her, had suffered a fatal heart attack two years back.

At least he'd been doing what he loved. Fishing. Knowing he'd died with a smile on his face had taught her to cherish each and every moment life offered—the good moments, anyway. A proviso she hadn't really considered for the past six months whilst Prince Bloody Charming was wrapping her round his duplicitous little finger.

She harrumphed, then squinted into the peasouper. Nope. Still couldn't see more than a metre or so. They should be getting closer now.

There'd been some lights a minute ago— Oh! Wait a minute. Her heart soared, then plummeted. Was that a *Christmas tree* glittering through the fog?

A lighthouse? Acceptable.

A Christmas tree as a beacon of hope? Nope. No way.

Not after what she'd seen under her own Christmas tree.

Correction.

Her former Christmas tree. The one she'd decorated to Rafael's exacting standards. Standards she'd thought she'd be embracing as her own right up until she'd realised they were double standards.

An uneasy feeling swept through her. One that was becoming a bit too familiar. Had she been so dazzled by her surgeon fiancé's fancy lifestyle that she'd failed to notice his 'love' lacked emotional depth?

She fuzzed out a raspberry. He'd wooed her straight and simple. Even the hardest of hearts would've melted with his golden spotlight shining upon them. The elf he'd been wooing under their Christmas tree had certainly looked enamoured.

Whatever.

That was then—this was now. Christmas tree or not, Bourtree Castle was where she was going to have to reinvent herself. Make herself a harder, less vulnerable, more man-savvy Audrey than the one who had existed seventy-two hours ago.

She looked down at her immaculate white down coat and grinned. The Ice Queen of Bourtree Castle. Perfect. She was ready to let the past go and let her new life begin.

She grabbed on to the railing with her mittened hands. She wouldn't be caught out when the boat lurched into place against the dock. She wouldn't be caught out by anything ever again.

'Nice outfit, Coop!'

'Black Friday special,' he shouted back to the dock worker, who laughed and gave him a jaunty salute before heading towards the end of the dock where the ferry was due any minute.

He had to hand it to the islanders. It had been a week since his gran's funeral, and not one person had yet to grind in the guilt that had enveloped him since she'd passed. There'd been a fair few queries about a wake, but he'd get there. Eventually.

Perhaps the collective tactic was to jolly him into paying his penance in the form of taking up Doc Anstruther's post when he retired. Or maybe—and far more likely—they were letting him stew in the sludge of his own mistakes while they got on with their lives.

Whatever. He couldn't worry about that now. He had a district nurse to collect and patients to see and joy to spread. He'd get a smile from each and every one of his patients if it killed him.

He gave his feet a stamp and his leather-gloved hands a brisk rub. Island cold was definitely different from mainland cold. A childhood on Bourtree should've made him immune to it but, despite the layers, fifteen years away from the island meant that today's wind was digging straight through to his bones.

His gran's voice came through clear as a bell. *'There's no such thing as bad weather, Coop, only bad clothing choices. Every day's fine as the next so long as you're dressed right.'*

His grandmother had had a truism for everything. Even him.

'Cooper, your problem is you're too busy looking to the future to notice the here and now. Stop and smell the roses, laddie. Otherwise the only thing you'll end up with is a life with no memories and no one to share it with.'

So here he was. Trying to make some good memories on Bourtree. Memories he wished like hell he could share with her.

He looked up the long cobbled lane that led to

the enormous Bourtree Castle Christmas tree. The castle ruins and the glittering tribute to Christmas spearheaded the small town square some twenty-odd metres above the docks. He gave the tree a respectful nod. He'd chosen it as a visual reminder that the Christmas spirit started at home and, like it or not, Bourtree was home. For the foreseeable future anyway.

A big man—muscular, not fat—wearing rugby shorts and a short-sleeved shirt walked up alongside him and the small crowd of folk waiting for the ferry coming in from Glasgow. *Strewth.* Shorts and a T-shirt in this weather? The man was either mad or Bourtree Castle through and through. Red hair, face covered in freckles, light blue eyes. Could be from any number of families on the island.

'Coop.' The guy gave him a nod and a smile.

'All right, mate?' Cooper replied, not at all sure what the man's name was.

He looked familiar. Had they been in the same class at school, or had Cooper seen him in one of his gran's stacks of local papers, fist in the air, cheering some sort of rugby triumph?

He still had a face full of acne… The cauliflower ear was new. As was the nose that looked to have been broken a few times and… yup…the scar cutting across his eyebrow. A scar mostly likely 'won' when the opposing team had crushed him at the bottom of a scrum pile.

It was a level of tough-as-nails that Cooper had never aspired to. Not that he shied away from sports. He went to the gym. Ran regularly. Did his weekly weights routine. But bulking up to get tangled in a pile of men who could throw a caber as easily as they could a toothpick? No, thanks. Fixing their compound fractures afterwards? Yeah. That was more his thing.

'Gone soft over there in Glasgow, have you?' the man asked, taking in Cooper's layered ensemble and foot-stamping.

'Hardly!' Cooper barked, despite the fact they both knew otherwise. 'Life on the mainland's like bootcamp in the arctic. Harder.'

The white lie dug the sharp knife he'd been carrying around in his ribs just that little bit deeper. Who the hell *was* this guy? He should know him. He squinted, stripped away the crinkles round the man's eyes, then tried to imagine him scrawny. That was it. He used to be scrawny.

'Robbie? Robbie Stuart?'

'Aye. Well done. Knew you'd get there in the end. Changed a bit, me, haven't I?' Robbie grinned, thumped his chest with one of his fists, then gave Cooper a proper thump on the back with the other. 'Good to have you back on the

island, even if—well—we're all missing her.
Your gran. Never met a woman with more spark
in her. Or more sense of community spirit—
specially this time of year. The Nativity'll never
be the same. Like herding cats to pull that thing
off, and she always did it. A tough-as-old-boots
islander through and through, Gertie was.'

'Aye, well…' He was trying to fill the Gertie
void as best he could, but growing up on Bourtree hadn't exactly been a bed of roses for him.
A change of topic might be in order.

'What sort of get-up do you call this?' He
tipped his head at Robbie's shorts and T-shirt
ensemble.

'It's my work gear, isn't it? I just finished a
PE session down at the college, then got a call
from my brother to come and pick up my wee
sister, as he's helping out Dad down the shop.'

Hearing about family members helping
family members as naturally as they breathed
should've been a heart-warmer. Especially this
time of year. Instead it dug that proverbial knife
in deeper still.

'Do you remember Rachel?' Robbie asked.
'She's living over in Glasgow now. A librar-
ian at a kiddies' school, but comes home twice
a month, rain or shine. Sometimes it takes a
bit of wrangling, what with her roster and her
boyfriend and all that, but she makes it work.'

Cooper, to his shame, neither remembered Rachel nor knew her routine. To say he hadn't been a regular on the Bourtree-Glasgow ferry would've been a massive understatement.

He'd spent most of his time on Bourtree plotting ways to get off the island, not back on it. Staying away had been a far easier way to avoid stories about his mum and dad. A car accident had taken them in the end. Little wonder with the way they'd regularly shirked the drink-driving laws.

Each time he had a patient suffering from liver failure, he thought of his parents and how they'd got off easy. It was a painful way to go.

'Speaking of get-ups…what's this for?' Robbie asked, tweaking the fabric of Cooper's jacket between his massive fingers. 'You preparing to throw yourself down some chimneys?' He laughed at his own joke.

'Picking up the new district nurse,' Cooper corrected.

'Oh, aye? Getting your foot in the door with Dr Anstruther, are you?'

'Just helping out.'

He was testing the waters. Seeing if working here would do something—anything—to ease his guilt over not having been here for his gran. The 'uniform' was as much a buffer for him as it was for the patients who might not be so keen to have the island bad boy turn up at their door with a doctor's case in hand.

He should've told Doc Anstruther he'd take the job the day he arrived. Made the decision as quickly and cleanly as a surgeon made an incision. He knew they were taking bets down at the pub about whether or not he'd stay.

It was a simple bet— would he stay or go? — but really he knew it went deeper. The decision he made would cement the way folk thought about the MacAskill name. Was he a good islander like his grandmother? Or a bad seed like his father? His sister had made her own decision by moving to New Zealand years back. Cooper had kept folk guessing long enough.

He knew opinions about him swung to both ends of the spectrum. Some thought his grandmother's firm but fair hand in raising him and his sister once their parents had died had made all the difference. Others weren't so generous.

A fair call, when being here tapped into his darker side. Anyway… He hadn't made the call and he wouldn't yet. He'd learnt the hard way about making promises he couldn't keep. If he made this promise he'd have to know in his marrow he was going to keep it. The intention was there. All he had to do now was see if he had the follow-through to ensure the island still had a 'good' MacAskill on it.

'Good to have you back for a wee while, Coop. And as Mr Holly Jolly himself, no less.' Robbie gave him another thump on the back. 'Brilliant. Your gran would've loved this, she would.'

Despite himself, Coop's lips curved into a half-smile as they both examined his outfit. His grandmother *would've* loved it. Thick black boots with a solid tread. Dark red trousers. A huge but lightweight jacket that fitted like a dream over his thermal top, wind-resistant fleece and gilet. Some might argue that the floppy hat with ermine lining was a bit OTT, but if there was a beautiful woman teasing him about it he'd flirtatiously suggest that it brought out the blue in his eyes.

But he was with Robbie, and not feeling remotely flirty. He was feeling antsy and guilty and quite a few other things he was used to shoving in a box to worry about when hell froze over.

He glanced at his watch. The ferry was making a real production of pulling in half an hour later than scheduled.

Fog.

Surprise, surprise.

'This the new regulation uniform, then, Coop?'

'For house calls,' Cooper said, playing it straight.

'Aye, well… I dare say folk'll appreciate the effort.'

'Hope so.'

And he did. Truly, he did. He might not be able to fix the way his gran had gone—alone—but he was going to pour every ounce of energy he had into making sure no one else's loved ones felt sad, or lonely, or any worse than they had to over the Christmas holidays. He'd chop down a Christmas tree for each and every one of them if necessary.

He jogged in place for a minute.

'What's this, then, Coop?' Robbie gave him a jab in the ribs. 'It's a bit late to get fighting fit for the new district nurse, isn't it? Bit of a hottie, is she?'

'No idea.'

Romance was the last thing on his mind. Another of his periodic relationships had bit the dust a few months back, and he'd been too busy working to think about it since. Too busy working to be here for his gran during what had turned out to be her final days. The promise he should've made to her years ago—that he'd make her proud of the man he'd become—he'd had to make over her grave.

'Never met her. I just hope she's a good nurse. We've got to go straight out on some calls.' He nodded out towards the car park, where the medical four by four stood ready and waiting.

Robbie's eyes opened in surprise. 'I still can't get my head wrapped round the fact Cooper MacAskill is doing calls on Bourtree. I thought you'd be too much of a bigshot over there in Glasgow for the likes of us.'

Cooper only just managed to keep his expression neutral. 'Doc's busy in the surgery, so I said I'd do the house calls and take the nurse on her first few sets of rounds.'

Robbie nodded. 'Someone down at the Puffin said you were doing a few days to help out Doc Anstruther, but I said I wouldn't believe it till I saw it. Cooper MacAskill on Bourtree?' He laughed, as if the idea was ridiculous.

Cooper gave his best stab at a nonchalant shrug, gritting his teeth against having his face rubbed in the past. A better reaction than connecting his fist to Robbie's nose, anyway. An instinct from back in the day.

If he decided to stay, punching people wouldn't exactly be kicking things off on the right note, so he took a deep breath, smiled, and prayed for the ferry to dock. Immediately.

Ach, well. If he decided to become the island's doctor he'd better get used to having these sorts of conversations. He owed it to Bourtree. More importantly, he owed it to his gran. Not that doling out aspirins and wrapping up sprained ankles while the doctors over in Glasgow got properly stuck into the type of emergency medicine he was trained for was his idea of heaven, but the simple truth was nothing could change the fact he'd not been by his gran's side when she had passed away.

Just a cold.

He should've known better. It was pneumonia season and, no matter how hale and hearty she'd been, older folk were always more vulnerable to contracting it after a virus. Particularly when they insisted upon riding their bicycles and paying house calls to elderly friends on a wintry Scottish island constantly cloaked in a shroud of cloud.

He should've been here. Driven her around. Brought her hot toddies and tea when the first round of sniffles hit. Nodded and smiled as she and her friends nattered on about needlepoint or whatever it was they talked about, whilst he daydreamed about life back in the A&E in Glasgow. He should have put an oxygen mask on her when she got short of breath.

'It's taking a wee while to find the mooring, isn't it?' Robbie nodded at the ferry, which was crawling towards the docks at a snail's pace.

A pace Cooper would've railed against if

it were an ambulance pulling into the bay at Glasgow Central.

'Island pace', his gran had called it.

Slow down, Coop. Nothing's going to change for the sake of an extra ten minutes.

That was what she hadn't understood. He'd been wired differently. Wired to respond to things in an instant. To a parent whose mood could turn on a dime. To an unkind child whose taunts might gain traction. A grandmother to please, a sister to protect, a reputation to—

Anyway… His ability to respond quickly meant A&E medicine suited him to a T. A seemingly innocuous situation could change to life-threatening in a matter of minutes. Seconds, even. A nicked artery. A septic wound.

A grandmother's cold shifting into pneumonia as her grandson made excuses, yet again, as to why he couldn't come back and have a wee look in on the woman who'd raised him when his own parents had fallen so short of the mark.

'So, when'll you be heading back to Glasgow?' Robbie asked as the ferry staff finally started securing the boat to the dock and a crowd of foot passengers began to gather out on deck to disembark.

'Good question,' Cooper said, eyes peeled for an unfamiliar face as the small crowd of regulars bowed their heads against the wind and headed for the car park or scanned the small group of folk he was standing amidst for a loved one. 'One I don't have an answer for.'

'What?' Robbie gave him a punch on the arm. 'I thought you would be high-tailing it back to the mainland as soon as Gertie's immediate affairs are settled. Even put money on it.'

Cooper felt the muscles in his jaw twitch. There had definitely been a time when he would've done that. But not after what he'd done. Not with the burden of guilt he now bore.

'Coop! MacAskill!'

Cooper looked up and saw one of the sailors pointing out a woman in an immaculate white ankle-length coat.

When his eyes landed on her face the wind was knocked out of him. And not because of the cold.

Dark brown almond-shaped eyes, the perfect shade of chocolate, met his straight on. A smattering of freckles made her look younger than he suspected she was. Somewhere around his age? Younger, more likely. Thirty to his thirty-five?

Her hair colour was a bit lighter than her eyes—a chestnut colour styled into an exacting pixie cut. As if she were a woodland faerie with a rulebook as long as her arm. Her overall aesthetic wasn't one that would've landed her at a modelling agency, but there was something about her that appealed to him at a core level. The upward tilt of her chin. The dubiously arched eyebrow.

The huge down jacket made her look expensive, but when he caught a glimpse of her nails as she clutched the coat round her neck he saw practically trimmed, clean nails rather than talons. She was a bit taller than average. Easy enough to pick up and carry over a threshold if she were— Hmm… Best not go there.

Her lips, bright red—from the cold, no doubt—were tipping into a frown. Just as he supposed his own mouth was.

For some reason he'd been expecting a sturdy, no-nonsense, silver-haired, woman who bustled. Most likely because that was exactly what Noreen, the woman she was filling in for, looked like.

Audrey Walsh was decades away from being silver-haired. Nor did she have the look of a bustler. She seemed more hustle than bustle. And, from the way she was giving him the side-eye, no nonsense to the core. Which was a good thing. This was the busy season—and he wasn't talking about Christmas parties.

Speaking of which… She didn't look remotely impressed by his effort to spread Christmas cheer to their patients. Which was a bad thing.

'Ho-ho-ho,' he said. 'Welcome to Bourtree Castle.'

Her nose wrinkled as she pasted on a wary smile. 'I got your text about needing to head straight out to some calls. I presume this…' she wiggled her fingers at his Santa outfit '…is going to come off before we get to work?'

A burst of fire flared hot in his chest. No way. This was for his gran. And a district nurse should know more than most that house calls were about far more than taking temperatures and heartrates.

'Nope. In fact…' He held up the clear bag in his left hand, waving his right hand as if he were presenting her with a free car rather than a fancy dress costume. 'I've got something here for you to put on before we head out.'

Audrey's expression turned icy. 'Not a chance.'

Perhaps the jacket she was wearing should've been a hint that she was more Snow Queen than one of Santa's cheery helpers. But the Snow Queen's heart had melted in the end, so…

He held up the costume again. 'Sure? It's thermal lined.'

CHAPTER TWO

'No,' AUDREY REPEATED. 'Absolutely not.'

This was not at all the escape from Christmas and heartbreak that she'd been hoping for when she'd accepted this post.

Her mental checklist had been simple.

A place as far away from London as possible. *Tick*.

No excessive Christmas decorations. Anywhere.

Fail.

A crusty old doctor.

Fail.

Epic fail, in fact.

Cooper MacAskill was jaw-droppingly gorgeous. Dark hair. Piercing blue eyes. Full, sensual lips. And he was dressed as Santa Claus. How could she hate all things Christmas when Sexy Santa was standing there offering her a chance to be his adorable elf? It was almost hilarious. And equally cruel.

Of all the tricks fate could've played on her, it had landed her on an island with a gorgeous, Christmas-loving doctor whose accent was already sending shivers of pleasure down her spine. This would absolutely *not* do.

'I'm not going to wear it. If you insist, I will turn around and get straight back on that ferry.'

And head back to…where, exactly? She had nowhere else to go to. And she'd signed a contract.

'What's wrong with it?'

Cooper looked genuinely perplexed. As if it hadn't even occurred to him she'd refuse or… and this was being generous…as if he cared what she thought. He gave her a scan that, once again, sent a stream of shivers down her spine.

'It looks like it'll fit.'

She hid her discomfort with a huff. 'I don't want to wear the elf costume, Mr Kringle.'

'That's *Dr* Kringle to you.'

Though there was a smile playing upon his lips, something flashed bright in his sapphire-blue eyes. A flare of will, daring her to contest him. Challenging her for trying to strip the joy from something he obviously held dear.

Why couldn't he hold something else dear? Like…erm…pre-guessing what someone's temperature was, or always having a medical run-bag that was immaculately kitted out. But, no.

She got a hot doctor whose passion was doing house calls dressed as Santa Claus.

A bit weird for someone the islanders were taking bets on about leaving... He seemed to be embracing Bourtree Castle's Christmas cheer as if he was going to stay here for ever. No matter what the odds were. So why couldn't she do the same? Be happy in the here and now?

Because she was completely *miserable*, that was why! She'd just been dumped. The life she'd thought she was living had turned out to be a mirage. A tinsel-laced, fairy-lit, holly-decked mirage. With mistletoe. Far too much mistletoe.

Cooper jiggled the elf costume, its candy-striped arms waving as they caught the sea breeze.

A despairing wail formed deep within her. She wasn't a killjoy. Honestly. She'd used to love Christmas as much as this guy seemed to. More, even! Just not this year.

Then she thought of the patients they'd be heading out to see as soon as this costume situation was settled. Housebound, mostly. Or very, very ill. Vulnerable. She could do it for them... She *should* do it for them. Wasn't helping people why she'd become a nurse in the first place?

Her resistance softened. Okay, fine. But only during business hours.

'I will wear the hat,' she acquiesced primly. 'But that's it.'

Cooper was adjusting his own hat and repositioning his big black belt round what had to be a pillow. It definitely wasn't his own belly. Not with that much movement.

When their eyes met again, she could've sworn he winked. Not a sexy wink. More like a complicit *thank you* wink. One that said he got it. He understood that her protest went beyond the realms of not wanting to look silly. It was strangely intimate. It made her feel vulnerable and safe all at the same time. As if she had, for the first time in her life, been properly seen.

'Right. Just a quick briefing,' he said, as if the moment hadn't happened. 'I'll be going out with you for the next week or so. Introducing you to folk, showing you how things work round here.'

'I can't imagine they're all that different from how they work anywhere else,' she griped.

She'd been hoping for some alone time. Precious minutes in between patients to howl lovelorn songs in the car with tears pouring down her cheeks. Or feisty 'I Will Survive'-type power ballads. Disliking this too-attractive-for-his-own-good doctor was becoming easier by the second. She glared at him. She bet he'd tune his radio to whatever channel played twenty-four-hour Christmas songs.

'Island folk don't take to change that easily,' he said, by way of an explanation.

'Well, nor do I, but sometimes you have to go with the flow, don't you?' Her thumb automatically moved to her bare ring finger. She caught Cooper's eyes snag on the movement. She scrambled to divert his attention. 'So…is this your year-round uniform?'

He cocked his chin to the side and smiled, one of his teeth catching on his full lower lip as he considered his response. When he finally answered, his voice was honest, straightforward, and annoyingly lovely to listen to.

'First time I've worn one. Nor am I a year-round resident.'

'Then why all the fuss? The costume, the introductions?'

Light glimmered then darkened in his eyes. Another shared moment she couldn't entirely put her finger on. It felt as if he was trying to tell her he was battling his own demons.

So…the space she was craving so much—he needed some, too.

'Here.' He deftly changed the topic, reached out and easily lifted one of her heavy duffel bags from the ground where she'd dropped them. 'I'll take this.'

He glanced at the bag. It was huge. Contained pretty much everything she owned.

'If I didn't know any better, I'd say you were running away from home.'

Their eyes met and meshed. Oh, *sugar.* He'd seen everything she'd been trying to hide. Caught a glimpse of the pain and grief she was trying to outrun. Something shifted in her chest. This locum posting was either going to be much harder than she'd anticipated or…because of whatever it was that had just passed between the pair of them…healing.

It was a powerful feeling. It made her want to reel back her lightning-fast assessment of 'Dr Kringle' and his love of Christmas costumes.

She rearranged her scarf, using the task to mask the fact she was actually checking him out as he did a quick flick through his phone's text messages. Not that she fancied him or anything. Obviously. Even so, she'd have to be blind not to notice he wasn't hard on the eye. If you liked tall, sparkly blue-eyed, ebony-haired men who dressed as Santa Claus. Which she didn't.

Because if she'd learned anything the hard way, it was that if something came wrapped up in a too-good-to-be-true package it *was* too good to be true.

Why did they have to be wrapped in Christmas cheer? Couldn't they just wear red scrubs, or their normal uniforms and spread joy the old-fashioned way? A smile, a thorough medical examination and a nice cup of tea?

Not that she'd done many house calls lately. Rafael had convinced her to start taking shifts at an elite paediatrics hospital. He'd said it gave the pair of them a 'better profile'. Silly her for thinking caring for people under any circumstances gave a good impression. What she did as a district nurse might not be showy, but it certainly improved the lives of those who received her visits.

'Eh, Coop!'

A huge man shouldering a neon pink duffel bag crossed to them and whacked Cooper on the back. Cooper held his ground. Blimey. He was made of stern stuff. Audrey would've gone hurtling to the floor with the amount of welly that had backed that friendly thwack.

'Who's this, then?'

Cooper shifted his stance, almost as if he was body-blocking the rugby player. Strangely protective for someone she'd just met and point-blank refused to play Holly Jolly Christmas with.

'Robbie Stuart,' he said, turning to her as he did so, 'meet our locum district nurse, Audrey…'

'Walsh,' she filled in. It would've been Audrey de Leon in twenty-three days and five hours' time, but…nope. 'Plain old Audrey Walsh.'

Cooper's eyes narrowed, as if he was clocking up another titbit of information about her. *Hates elf costumes. Running away from her life and thinks her name is boring.*

She popped on a smile. 'Shall we go and see some patients?'

'Good idea. Robbie…' Cooper gave him a goodbye nod.

'You should come down to the Puffin tonight,' Robbie called after them. 'A whole bunch of us'll be meeting up after the Nativity rehearsal for a wee drink. Folk'll be dying to meet you—see if they can rope you into helping now that— Sorry, Coop.'

Audrey threw a questioning look in Cooper's direction.

'The Nativity's an annual island tradition,' he explained. 'Don't go if Christmas isn't your thing. As for the "wee drink" part—the whole of Bourtree will most likely be there, especially once news has travelled that you've arrived. New arrivals are always big news here on Bourtree.'

'A bit like the bets on whether you're going to stay or not?'

The moment she said it, she knew she'd made a mistake. His blue eyes darkened and a barely disguised flinch whipped the smile from his lips.

Why had she stuck her foot in it right when they'd seemed to be developing the tiniest sliver of camaraderie?

'Sorry. I— It's none of my business.'

'No, no.' Cooper shook his head, gave Robbie a half-wave and began heading towards the car without so much as an attempt to meet her apologetic face. 'Everything's fair game on Bourtree. You'll learn that soon enough, too.'

'Sounds ominous.'

He gave a shrug that all but screamed, *That's life, kid. Get used to it.*

He did have a point. Though she'd already been through all her ex's faults with a fine-tooth comb, she was pretty certain *she* had some home truths that needed examining. Not to mention the warning signs in their relationship that she should've heeded. Like the whole 'no personal possessions around the flat' thing. As if they lived in a show home and making it appear remotely homely would weaken their stance as a power couple.

If this was only easing open the can of worms labelled *Warning Signs*…she was scared to pull the lid entirely open.

Cooper opened the back of a brightly marked medical four-by-four parked further up the dock, slung her bag on top of a gurney, then the smaller tote that she'd been carrying behind it. He closed the doors and turned to her, his eyes sparking. Maybe from some sort of unspent fury or…maybe it was the lights from the Christmas tree.

It was hard to tell. Same as her, she supposed. Two people treading the fine line between contentedness and fury that life hadn't turned out the way they'd planned. When he spoke, she knew straight away that what she'd seen had come from somewhere dark.

'Some people try to outrun their demons. Some run straight into their arms. I meet my challenges head-on. Now, let's go see some patients.'

'I'm sorry to be rushing out the door like this,' the young mum said. 'I've got to pick up the kiddies from school and get their tea on at home. I'll come back when Deacon's home from work and can look after the wee ones, but I'll have to shoot off again for the Nativity rehearsal.'

'Do you have a good role?' Audrey asked.

The first smile they'd seen from Mhairi since they'd arrived surfaced. 'Brilliant role. I'm Frigg.'

Audrey looked at Cooper. *Frigg?* Not one of the usual cast of characters she was used to in a Nativity.

He gave a little *I'll tell you later* shake of the

head, then addressed Mhairi—'An auld Scots name pronounced Vah-ree,' Cooper had explained as they'd waited for her to answer the door.

He told her that they'd look after her father and would ring her with any updates.

Mhairi threw an anxious look back towards her father's bedroom, then tugged her hand through her thick batch of wayward curls. 'It's difficult taking you seriously, Coop.'

'Why? I'm still me beneath all this.'

He lifted his Santa hat off his head as if to prove it. A thick, wavy black head of hair that reached his collar was revealed. If anything, the 'reveal' seemed to make him a little bit less mortal and Audrey a bit more wary. Mhairi, too, from the dubious sound she was making.

'I suppose so. It's just that…well…we're so used to Dr Anstruther or Noreen coming out. I mean, they're just a bit more familiar with everything…so I don't worry so much when I have to go.'

Cooper nodded, trying to keep his expression neutral. He'd encountered this attitude more than once over the past week. Sure, everyone knew he was an A&E doctor over on the mainland, but no one had actually seen him in scrubs. Performing a tracheotomy. Calling for a crash cart when someone flat-lined, only to bring them back to life before it arrived.

No. They'd seen him hauled out of fights in the school yard. Racing a motorcycle he had been too young to ride. Playing truant. And because of that he'd have to earn their trust, centimetre by painful centimetre. It was a job that could take years. Years of patience he wasn't sure he had the reserves for. But today he had it. And that was what counted.

'Mhairi, I know you're worried, but we will look after your dad to the best of our abilities. I am still a doctor underneath all this Santa gear. And Audrey here is one of the finest nurses London has to offer. If the two of us can't figure out how to help him, we'll get Doc Anstruther out to have a look after surgery—all right?'

Despite the gravity of the situation, and Mhairi's obvious concern for her father, Audrey felt a little tug of pride that Cooper was already assuring one of the islanders that they could trust her. It wasn't as if he'd seen anything beyond her CV. Maybe all that prickly interaction down at the docks had been a case of miscommunication. A false start.

Mhairi tugged on the coat she'd taken off the back of a wooden chair. 'I'd stay if I could, but I'm already running late.' She made a frustrated sound. 'He's not at all his usual self,' she continued, scooping up a pair of car keys. 'I've never known him to not get out of bed. That's why I rang. I always come by for a cuppa and some shortbread before I pick up the little ones, and he's usually pottering about the place, fussing about with whatever project he's been working on, but he's still in bed. Said he's not been out since yesterday. Blinds drawn…everything.'

Cooper helped her pull her jacket into place. A gentlemanly gesture he performed as if it had been drilled into him from an early age.

'Bed might be the best place for him if he's feeling poorly, Mhairi. If we think he needs to be in hospital we'll get him there.' He named a premier hospital in Glasgow and said he had some contacts there who would be sure to give him the best care if it was anything serious.

Mhairi froze, hands gripping her collar. 'But—that's over on the mainland.'

There was the aversion to change Cooper had mentioned, thought Audrey.

'Aye, but there'll be folk there to look after him round the clock. It'll take some of the pressure off you. It's a good hospital.'

'Is it the one where you work?' Mhairi asked.

'I know it well and can recommend it.'

Interesting, Audrey thought. That wasn't really an answer.

Mhairi shook her head and dropped her keys back onto the table. 'I don't like the idea of it. Especially over Christmas. The folk there won't know him. And he'd hate it, being away from us and the grandkids. We're all he has.'

The sentiment spoke to Audrey loud and clear. *Family.* It was something she'd always ached for—especially as a little girl, growing up in the shadow of her father's grief over their shared loss of her mother.

'You know what it's like to have to fend for yourself, Coop,' Mhairi said. 'It's not nice.'

Cooper gave his jaw a scrub and said nothing, but an electric tension Audrey couldn't put her finger on crackled between the two.

'Sorry, Cooper...' Mhairi put up her hands in apology, then dropped them. 'I didn't mean anything by that.'

'I know.'

An awkward silence hummed between them as he picked up her car keys and handed them to her, effectively ending the exchange.

Audrey jumped in, feeling a protective impulse to cover for Cooper's silence. Whatever was going on with him, he wasn't comfortable talking about it, and that was definitely something she could relate to.

'No one's going anywhere right now. Our job is to try and keep your father out of hospital.

Why don't you let us get on with our examination and we'll let you know as soon as possible how things stand?'

'How long will you be here?' Mhairi's eyes darted between Cooper and Audrey.

'Five weeks,' Audrey said.

'No,' Cooper corrected with a soft smile. 'She means today.'

Ah. In that case...

Audrey gave Cooper a *This is your call* look. She knew they had other patients to see. Back in London she would've raced from patient to patient as best she could, willing there to be more hours in the day, but perhaps things worked differently here. The part of her that needed to know compassion still existed hoped that Cooper would say they'd stay as long as necessary—without, of course, compromising any other patient's health.

'Your father won't be left on his own if we have any critical concerns,' Cooper said solidly.

Another piece of Audrey's heart softened for him. A dangerously slippery slope if she didn't watch herself.

'Promise?'

Audrey didn't miss the look that passed between them when Cooper promised. It was as if he was staking his personal reputation on the commitment. No patient left unattended, no matter what. It was a big promise to make. Particularly when they had other patients to see.

'You'd better get on away down the road. School'll be over soon.'

Mhairi opened the kitchen door, took a step out, then turned back. 'You know, on second thought, I think I'll bring the little ones back here—unless you think he's got something infectious. They can have their tea in front of the telly as a special treat, and that way I can keep an eye on Dad.'

Cooper gave her a nod. 'Fair enough. We'll call you.'

The way he said it put an end to the matter, but in a kind way. Mhairi's father would get the care he needed. End of discussion.

When she'd left, he turned around and nodded towards the bedroom door. 'Right then, Audrey. Let's see what you're made of.'

A few minutes later, after running through the elderly gentleman's medical history and conducting a few preliminary checks, Cooper found his concerns were as high as his daughter's had been. Audrey's too, if her furrowed brow was anything to go by.

Glenn Davidson, their octogenarian patient, was not in a good way. He had a fever, was dehydrated, had low concentration and was very weak. They'd ruled out flu, as he didn't have any congestion or a sore throat. The fatigue and fever he was feeling was something he'd felt creeping up on him rather than something that had hit him in a blast, as flu symptoms often did. Besides, he'd assured them, he'd had a flu inoculation back in September.

'Had it right before your grandmother, I did,' Glenn had said weakly, rocking back and forth on the edge of the bed as if the movement was literally jogging his memory. 'We'd made the appointments together so we could swap magazines.'

Audrey's eyes shot to Cooper.

He looked away.

He'd not mentioned the glaring scarlet letter on his chest to her. A for abandonment. Perhaps he should have. But there was a part of him that was grateful that a new colleague meant a clean slate. She had no idea who he was and vice versa. Yet another chance to try and be the man he'd always hoped to be. Honourable. Loyal. Kind.

Moments like these were pointed reminders that he had quite a journey ahead of him before hitting any of those milestones. He'd known about Gran's flu shot, so hadn't been worried— but, like Mr Davidson here—his gran had been elderly, making her more vulnerable to chest infections.

Pneumonia didn't care whether or not you'd had a flu inoculation.

He should've been more like Mhairi, moving his world around to be there for her. His gran had been the woman who'd protected him all his life, and what had he done? Spread his wings, as she'd taught him, then flown too far from the nest to be of any use.

'Any history of Alzheimer's?' Audrey asked in a low voice.

Ah. A simple question, not an accusatory glance. He'd have to start checking his guilty conscience at the door if he was going to get through the day with his focus where it needed to be: on his patients.

Cooper shook his head in the negative, then busied himself with jotting down a few notes on Mr Davidson's chart. He would tell Audrey what had happened when they were done here. It would put all the little asides everyone was bound to make in context. Besides, there'd been something in Audrey's eyes that had given him reason to believe she had her own set of troubles. Who knew? Maybe she'd understand and he'd have an ally.

And maybe a kangaroo would bounce into the room and wish them all a happy Christmas.

'Is that too snug?' Audrey looked into Glenn's watery blue eyes as she adjusted the blood pressure cuff.

'No, it's fine,' Glenn said, not sounding entirely convinced—or focused, to be honest. His attention had dipped in and out ever since they'd entered his bedroom. Although in fairness, Cooper's had, too.

He'd suggested Audrey take the lead, so he could get a feel for how she worked, but she seemed a bit edgy. As if his decision was less a vote of confidence and more an opportunity for him to loom over her, judging her every move.

She popped her stethoscope ear-tips into place, gave the instrument's metal head a bit of a rub between her hands, so it wasn't cold, then gave the inflation bulb a quick pump to see whether or not Glenn's blood pressure was as low as they suspected.

As she put the stethoscope bell to his forearm he began to droop forward. Cooper was there in an instant, helping her right him. 'Easy there, Mr Davidson. I've got you.'

The poor man was finding it hard to sit upright, and started muttering something about finding the dog…the dog would help. So far as he knew, Glenn hadn't had a dog for some years. Maybe that Alzheimer's diagnosis should be reconsidered.

'Shall we rearrange your pillows there, Glenn? Let you lie back in bed? Is it dizziness you're feeling or fatigue?'

'Both. I don't understand what's happening,' Glenn said, for about the tenth time since they'd propped him up in his bed and begun the examination. 'Can't wrap my head round it.'

'Is this normal for him?' Audrey whispered to Cooper.

That increasingly familiar blaze of defensiveness charged through him. He didn't know the ins and outs of every single human on Bourtree. No one did. Except, perhaps, his gran and Dr Anstruther, who'd been here over forty years. And Mhairi. And the neighbours. And, and, and…

But this wasn't about him. This was about Glenn.

He knelt down on one knee so that he could look directly into Mr Davidson's eyes. 'Glenn. We weren't able to have much of a talk with Mhairi when we arrived as she was late picking up the children. Are you able to explain exactly what's bothering you?'

'Hurts,' he said.

Cooper's eyes darted from the blood pressure cuff to Audrey, then back to Glenn.

'The cuff? Glenn, you've got to say if it pinches, all right? No prizes for bravery today.'

'No, it's more…' Glenn drew his knees up towards his chest.

'Glenn?' Audrey asked as she swiftly released the cuff from his arm. 'Are you eating at all?'

He shook his head. 'Nah. Not hungry.'

'Have you been sick?'

'Nah. Nah. I just want to sleep. Or die.' He fell back into the mound of pillows they'd built behind him and closed his eyes against whatever invisible pain he was enduring.

'Have you been drinking plenty of water?'

Glenn gave a soft moan and muttered something about a wee nip being all he could manage and it had only been to try and stop the pain.

Cooper winced. Alcohol wasn't a brilliant solution to anything. In fact, it wasn't a solution at all.

Cooper's heart went out to him as his brain whizzed through all the possibilities and prayed to whatever gods were out there that his grandmother had never felt this low. Doc Anstruther had said she'd gone in her sleep. It had been little comfort to him, but seeing Glenn like this, in agony, he was grateful for the small mercy she'd been shown.

Audrey's eyes locked on Cooper's and the wheels were obviously turning behind those brown eyes of hers. The expression on her face made it clear she knew very well that this was definitely not the psychological terrain you wanted any patient to be treading.

Audrey gave her forehead a little scratch, then asked, 'How often are you going to the toilet, Glenn?'

Glenn looked at her, his eyes lucid for the first time since they'd entered the room. 'All the time. I stopped drinking water yesterday, because it was getting to be too much, and I didn't want to wear…you know…nappies for men.'

Audrey gave his hand a gentle squeeze. Cooper appreciated the gesture. Getting an older man to talk about intimate things such as hygiene and incontinence was tough. Particularly when he was a Scottish Islander. He'd been told once that each male bairn born to the island received the same welcome upon their first cry. *A good hearty voice you have, laddie, now that'll be enough of that.*

Glenn's voice lowered to a whisper. 'I barely made it back to bed the last time, before I had to turn round and go back.'

As one, Cooper and Audrey figured it out. UTI.

He gave her a nod that said, *You go ahead.*

'I think you've got yourself a bad urinary tract infection, Glenn,' Audrey said, catching eyes again with Cooper.

He gave a little *Of course it is* thunk to his

forehead, out of Glenn's line of vision. He should've added up the symptoms. Discomfort. Fever. Distractedness. Pain.

'What does that mean?' Glenn asked.

'It means we can get you feeling much more like yourself with some antibiotics,' Audrey said with a gentle smile.

Cooper nodded. That was a great way to deal with a patient. Let them know the prognosis was good first, then let them know how it would happen.

'Will it be instant?'

'No,' Cooper said when Audrey threw him a *Help, please* look. 'But if we get some fluids into you and ask your daughter to pick up the prescription on her way over, after picking up your grandkids, you should be feeling better by morning and better still in a few days' time.'

'Don't you need to take samples or anything?'

'Aye, we will, Glenn—if you're up to it. But, as Audrey pointed out, all your symptoms add up to a classic UTI. They can drive men mad. You should be proud you've made it this far without hallucinating.'

Glenn barked out a laugh. 'I thought I was when *you* walked through the door, Coop.'

'Eh?'

Glenn waved a trembling finger in his direction. 'This get-up you're wearing. I thought Santa had come to take me away to my maker.'

Audrey tried and failed to squelch a smile.

'Thought I'd spread some Christmas cheer a bit early this year. Looks like I brought some Christmas fear instead.'

Glenn's clear-eyed look softened. 'I'd like to make it to Christmas.'

'Eh, well.' He gave the man's thin shoulder a gentle pat. 'You'll make it well past Christmas and Hogmanay, if Audrey and I have anything to do with it.'

'But you'll not be here for any follow-up,' Glenn said, the lift in his mood instantly plummeting. 'If I make it through to the New Year, that is. And of course Dr Anstruther will be off in the tropics somewhere...'

Audrey looked up at Cooper. This was his question to answer. Her contract lasted through until New Year's Day. He didn't have a contract. Not yet.

'Noreen'll be back, Glenn. She'll keep her watchful eye on you. Don't you worry. You'll be skipping through the spring heather before you know it.'

'Aye...' Glenn cracked a smile, then closed his eyes. 'That'll be right.'

'Right, Glenn,' Audrey said, adroitly sensing

the older man's need for some rest. 'Let me pull this lovely blanket up around you.'

As Audrey pulled a brightly coloured blanket up around him Cooper's heart skipped a beat. There was only one person on the whole of Bourtree who would've put together a blanket with that colour scheme. Gertie MacAskill. His gran.

Luckily, Audrey missed the hit of recognition as she was too busy tucking it into place.

'Why don't we get you some water to have by your bed, Glenn? Is there any particular glass you like?'

He muttered something indecipherable as she moved away from his bedside and she and Cooper left the room.

'Good call on the UTI,' Cooper said as he popped his medical bag on the kitchen table and put everything back in order. 'You got there before I did.'

'I'm sure that's not true,' Audrey said, then added, 'I used to see them all the time amongst my older patients and he has pretty classic symptoms.'

'Used to?'

Audrey looked away, busying herself with opening cupboards to find a glass. 'I took a job at a children's hospital a couple of months back.

It was great, of course, but there's a different sort of job satisfaction from district nursing.'

There was something in that admission, he thought. Guilt? Loss? Hard to put his finger on it. Maybe something had happened on one of her calls that had made her switch to a hospital. Some people found the intimacy of being in a patient's home too much. He was one of them.

'I don't know. Diagnosing UTIs isn't as exciting as a bustling hospital.'

'All my patients receive the same treatment,' Audrey bit out as she filled the glass with water over a pile of unwashed dishes in the kitchen sink. 'Whether they're at home or anaesthetised and about to go into surgery.'

Okay. Cool your jets.

'I wasn't suggesting otherwise.'

She set the glass down on the counter, then pulled on a pair of washing up gloves that hung over the tap.

'What are you doing?'

'What does it look like I'm doing?' She put the tap on full and gave the dishes beneath a big squirt of washing up liquid.

'Doing dishes isn't the normal remit of a district nurse.'

She looked at him as if his heart was made of stone. 'Cooper, the poor man's unwell. His daughter sounds like she has less time than either of us do and—' she held up three coffee mugs, then dropped them back into the soapy water '—these might offer some insight as to why Glenn's suffering. It looks like he's had nothing but coffee, whisky and…from the looks of this plate…a curry ready-meal. None of which are any good for a UTI. Offering him advice on what is and isn't going to help him feel better is very *much* the remit of a district nurse.'

Well, that was him told. And fair enough, too.

Cooper scrubbed a hand over his stubbly chin, hoping the conciliatory sound he'd just made would make up for the fact that he was wrong and she was right.

The truth was, he was only a handful of days into this house doctor gig and he was still trying to find the job's heartbeat. When he'd come back to Bourtree, Dr Anstruther had met him at the docks to drive him up to his gran's. He'd ever so casually mentioned that he was retiring on Christmas Eve and that he had the budget for another doctor up until then. It was intended to go to the doctor who'd be replacing him, but as there weren't any takers so far…

He'd refused at first. Said this was a one-doctor island. But Doc Anstruther had said there were a few cases he might find interesting. So far they'd yet to surface. And if anything truly disastrous happened, an air ambulance and doctors from the mainland would be flown in. They'd flown in for his parents. Too late, as it happened, but they'd been part of the inspiration for Cooper to become a doctor. Helping when people needed help most. Commanding instant trust. Respect.

Two things he didn't know if he would ever earn here.

He gave the back of his head a rub. What was done was done. Enough introspective soul destruction for one day. Luckily he had a perfect distraction in the form of an anti-elf-suit, pixie-haired district nurse, who'd left the bright lights of London to come here to Bourtree. Maybe she could throw some light on what made this type of medical practice more desirable than working in a hospital.

He pulled the top over his run-bag and began to zip it shut. 'I'm curious,' he said. 'Why didn't you try another discipline after paediatric nursing rather than take a professional move backwards?'

Her eyes widened. 'Who says district nursing is going backwards?'

Oh, hell. Talk about open mouth and insert foot.

Cooper backtracked. 'Sorry. I'm not dissing it. Not at all. It's a valuable service. But c'mon…

Now that you've had a taste of it, you have to admit that life in a hospital is...'

He was about to say *the ultimate buzz* but he stopped himself. Getting an adrenaline hit out of other people's misfortunes wasn't what he meant. An ideal emergency department would be an empty one, but being a busy doctor with a non-stop flow of anonymous patients demanded full focus. Consumed more hours of the week than any other job he could think of. Hours spent improving people's lives, not destroying them, as his parents used to tell him over and over.

'If it hadn't been for you and your sister...'

The lives they would've led...

He cleared his throat and chose a simpler, less emotionally toxic tack. 'I'm just curious as to why you took this locum post rather than one at a London hospital. They pay better. There must be scores of jobs over Christmas if that's the goal. And yet you chose to come here. Why?'

From the look on Audrey's face, Cooper had done an *out of the frying pan into the fire* manoeuvre. So much for trying to steer clear of emotional toxicity.

'Not everything's about money and status, Dr *Claus.*'

She gave him a proper glare that tugged at an impulse to pull her into his arms and comfort her. Then, as quickly as her temper had flared, her lips curved into a weak but apologetic smile.

'Sorry. Touchy subject.'

'Money or status?'

'Neither.'

'A boyfriend obsessed with one or both?' he parried.

She chewed on the inside of her cheek. Whether she was fighting tears or conjuring up an acidic response to a question that was none of his business was difficult to tell. When she released it, he realised her lips were shaped like a perfect bow. A crimson bow that, if he were looking for a pair of lips to kiss, would be very inviting indeed.

'Something like that,' she said finally.

His eyes were still glued to her lips as she asked, 'Should we wrap up here and get to the next patient?'

There was a challenge in her tone. A dare for him to try and press her for more information. Fair enough. Calling his own love-life chequered would be putting it nicely.

He dragged his eyes away from her lips and took the glass of water to give to Glenn, doing his best to ignore the spark of connection when their hands brushed. He took the glass through to Glenn, made sure he was tucked up in bed, and gave him a reminder that they or his daughter would be back within an hour or so with his prescription, but to call if he needed anything.

When he got back to the kitchen Audrey was already heading to the car.

Fair enough.

He didn't like being pushed for answers to uncomfortable questions either. Why didn't he have a girlfriend? Why wasn't he married? Why didn't he have a family of his own when so many of his peers were already looking forward to their second or third child?

Questions people on Bourtree had never bothered asking him because they already knew the answers.

CHAPTER THREE

FOUR HOURS, ONE huge serving of takeaway fish and chips and seven patients later, Audrey and Cooper finally wrapped up the last of the calls. It was almost eight o'clock and, despite her cosy winter coat—now stained with mud, a streak of spilt tea and some errant ketchup from a friendly toddler—she was feeling the cold. The car's heating system had packed up after their second visit.

She could do with getting to her accommodation and slipping into a nice hot bath. Bubbles, a milky cup of tea and a chance to think about her busy day. Bliss. Although sitting down meant she might also think about the fact that she'd just had her heart crushed, her bank account devastated and, in five weeks' time, would have nowhere to live and no job to go to.

Cooper pulled the car onto the island's main road—there was only the one main coastal route, with loads of little twisty lanes shooting off it—to head back to the surgery, where she'd caught a fleeting glimpse of Dr Anstruther earlier in the day. So that she'd be in a better head space when she met him, she kept her dark thoughts at bay by making mental notes on each of their patients, most of whom they would see again either tomorrow or the next day.

On top of a couple of paediatric calls for some utterly adorable babies—one of whom had a questionable chest infection—there was another elderly patient, bed-bound courtesy of Parkinson's, a twenty-something chap with compound fractures in each of his femurs from a skiing mishap, a stubborn 'remote IT consultant', who was refusing to believe diabetes was the reason behind the circulatory problems in his feet, and a heartbreaking case of a young mum who was losing her battle with metastic bone cancer and whose only dream was to make it through to Christmas so that she didn't 'spoil it' for her children.

The selflessness of the comment had brought tears to her eyes and sent Cooper straight out through the door on what she was pretty sure had been a pretend errand for 'some paperwork'. Proof, at least, that the man had a heart.

No. That wasn't fair. He had proved himself to be an excellent doctor, slightly shifting his demeanour to suit each patient. She had no doubt he'd be brilliant in a busy A&E ward, every bit the professional, and now that she had spent some time with him she was no longer remotely attracted to him. Nope. Not one bit.

She hadn't even considered tucking an errant wave of his dark hair behind one of his ears. Or spent one idle moment wondering what it would be like to run her finger along his stubble to see if it was soft or rough to the touch. Nor had she even once considered what it would be like to touch his lips with her own. One hundred percent not at all.

Any emotional sparks that had flown had been likely due to her hypersensitivity about... well...*everything*.

If only wedding insurance paid out when the groom turned out to be a lying cheat. If only wedding insurance could erase your memory and let you start your adult life all over again— or at least from the point where she'd finally decided to sell the small house where she and her father had lived. That had been the moment when she'd begun to lose sight of herself, as if the house and all its memories, had anchored her to the woman she'd thought she was. The woman she'd wanted to become.

Rafael had actually laughed when she'd told him what it had sold for. It had been a lot to her, but her modest nurse's salary hadn't prevented it from falling into the 'fixer-upper' category. She'd put half of the money into a pension that she couldn't touch for years to come and then, like a complete and utter fool, she'd poured the rest of it into the wedding.

Rafael only liked the finest things in life, and for once she would be able to give him the very finest. What did it matter, she'd thought, if she spent all the money on their one special day? They'd be pooling resources after they were married and her splurge would make memories for a lifetime.

Nightmares, more like.

It was money she now desperately needed for a deposit on a flat somewhere—rented or otherwise—and to get on with her life. Without it she was right royally screwed. But keeping that shame to herself was critical if she wanted to leave here with her dignity intact. Not easy when she was busy biting Cooper's head off for his comments about money and status.

She owed him an apology on that front. He wasn't to know it had been Rafael who had encouraged her to leave her post as a district nurse. It shamed her now, how quickly she'd leapt at all his suggestions. Changing jobs. Moving in together. Planning a discreet but ultra-lush wedding away from prying eyes...

They'd decided on a tropical island in the end.

Staying in one of those amazing houses on stilts above an azure sea. First-class airline tickets. Spa treatments. Champagne on arrival. The lot.

It physically pained her how eager she'd been to please him. She'd been the shy, mousey type her whole life, and Rafael was the polar opposite. Assured, socially confident, and completely aware that his place in the world was amongst the upper echelons.

Maybe that had been it…the reason he'd cheated. She'd been too lowly for him. He'd wanted to pull a Prince Charming on her when she'd been quite happy being Cinderella before the ball—minus the stepsisters, obviously.

'You've done well today,' Cooper said, apropos of nothing.

A warm hit of appreciation bloomed in her chest. A welcome heat, as it was bloody freezing in his car.

'It's nice getting to know people in their home environment,' she said. 'I know paramedics and A&E docs are often seen as the real frontline, but I always like to think house call doctors and district nurses are the true healthcare SAS.'

'How so?' Cooper asked, sounding genuinely interested.

She flushed a bit when he nodded at her to go ahead. It was something she could be a bit too passionate about…but what the heck? She'd be gone in five weeks, and it wasn't as if she was going to be falling into his arms any time soon—or ever—so... 'Being in a patient's house makes a big difference in helping diagnose certain health problems.'

'In what way?' he asked. 'I find the less I know the person, the easier it is to be clinical about a diagnosis.'

She made a thoughtful noise, but then shook her head. 'That just makes it easier to make the hard decisions.'

Cooper nodded. 'Go on.'

'I think knowing a person and the environment they live in gives you a much better grounding for understanding a patient. It's easier to sift through to the real problem.'

'How's that?'

'Well,' she said. 'Take Jimmy, for example.'

'Jimmy Tarbot?'

He was the diabetic patient they'd seen earlier. He was about her age and, despite the fact he was facing potential amputation of his toes, he refused to acknowledge the fact that what he ate really did make a difference—that his diabetes wasn't just a case of 'bad genes'.

'Yes. He's obviously in denial about how bad his diabetes is.'

'He lets us come in and give insulin shots on a daily basis.'

'Yes, but…' Audrey didn't want to step on any toes here. 'It's a guaranteed visit from the outside world, isn't it?'

Cooper gave her a quick look. 'Go on,' he said again.

'He says he wants us to do the jabs because he has a fear of needles, but did he seem remotely freaked out to you?'

Cooper took a beat before answering in the negative.

'So,' Audrey continued, 'he's obviously hungry for company, but he isn't making any visible changes to make sure his health changes and he won't need the injections. Which is a little weird for someone who has a fear of needles, don't you think?'

'He told me he was on fruit and veg. Lean meat. The whole nine yards.'

'Did you look in his bin?'

'No.'

'There were several bakery bags in there, as well as a pink box which looked suspiciously like a cake box to me. Talbot's Bakery and Café? That's on the High Street, isn't it?'

Cooper nodded. 'Aye. But he says he doesn't go out. That's why we make these calls rather than give him injections down at the clinic. Because he's housebound.'

'Oh, I believe he doesn't go out. But not necessarily because he can't.' Audrey began ticking things off her fingers. 'There's absolutely nothing around his car to indicate it's left the drive recently. The refrigerator only has a pint of milk and a loaf of white bread in it. When I asked him about it, he said he gets one of the lads from the market to drop his shopping by on his way home. I'm guessing that's a trip via the bakery. Plus,' she added with a playful smirk, 'he told me when I asked him. About the needles. That he fakes being afraid of them.'

'I should've bought you a detective's hat—not an elf's hat.' Cooper flashed her a smile. It was so warm and genuine, it caught her off guard. As if she'd been hit by an actual ray of sunshine. 'I have to say, Audrey—and this is no offence to Noreen—but I can see why he'd fake a fear of needles if a beautiful woman like you was calling in on him on a daily basis. Who knows what he tells Noreen?'

She flushed right up to her hairline. The last thing she'd felt over the past few days was beautiful. Having the comment come from Cooper felt special. He certainly didn't seem the type to dole out compliments like candies. Then again…the man was wearing a Santa suit.

Audrey tried shrugging it off. 'I'm leaving soon. Sometimes it's easier to tell a complete stranger the truth rather than have the people you care about knowing about your vulnerabilities.'

She'd run for the hills as soon as her life had fallen to pieces. Hadn't told a soul. Packed her bags and left. Here, within such a close-knit community, it would be awful to feel ashamed of how or who you were.

'Do you think there's anything else that's keeping him hidden away in his house?'

Cooper thought for a minute, then said. 'I remember Jimmy from school. Shy as a mouse, he was. Would barely meet your eye when you talked to him. Everyone called him Big Jimmy, and he never seemed to mind, but maybe...'

'What?'

'Well, I think he struggled to find his "crew". He was never one for team sports. Always playing computer games and coding. Although he was in with the drama students for a while. Working backstage and such. That sort of thing.'

'Perhaps he's too embarrassed to go out. Never developed a thick skin against the name calling. Can you imagine what it must feel like to go out, knowing everyone is judging your weight, and wanting nothing more than to buy cake?'

'No one likes to be judged.'

Cooper's dark change of tone was so abrupt

Audrey felt a bit shocked. Was he speaking from experience?

He gave her a quick glance, then faced the road again. 'I still don't see what any of this has to do with a better diagnosis.'

Audrey huffed out a sigh. Wasn't it obvious? 'Now that we know he's not actually afraid of needles, we need to find ways to get him out of the house. Get him active.'

Cooper laughed. 'You like a challenge, don't you?'

'What do you mean?'

'You're going to try and change a man's habits? A man who's not left his house in years maybe? It's not easy to change a well-worn routine.'

'There are plenty of reasons why a person might change their routine,' she replied hotly, knowing her answer was fuelled by the fact that the night she'd found Rafael and his lover she'd been meant to be home late. She'd come home early from a regular girls' night out to surprise him, little knowing she'd be the one getting the surprise.

Cooper was drumming his fingers on the steering wheel, then he gave it a thump. 'I can see where you're coming from, but I'd be willing to lay down money that you'll not convince him to change his ways.'

She yanked her seat belt away from her chest and whirled on him. 'What *is* it with you? One minute you're all nice and complimentary, and the next you're taking little jabs, trying to cut me down.'

'Hey! Whoa.' Cooper pulled the car over to the side of the road. 'I'm trying to get to know you. Figure out how you think.'

And making a right hash of it.

'Oh, I see, Santa. Is this for your naughty and nice list? Or is it some sort of special island greeting? Building a person up, then tearing them down for your own amusement.'

He stopped himself from answering that question in the nick of time.

She was right, to an extent. He'd had a sharp tongue as a boy, and it hadn't been entirely smoothed as an adult. It was the main reason he'd been deemed 'not suitable' management material. Which was fine. He was an 'in the trenches' type of doctor. Even so, saying *exactly* what he thought wasn't always the wisest course of action. But when you'd been raised in a house where your own parents had freely informed you that they wished you'd never been born...

It was no excuse to be unkind. He needed all the allies he could get right now. Audrey was a lovely, hard-working woman who clearly wanted to do the very best for their patients. It was inevitable that she saw things from a different angle. And he'd been nothing but bloody awkward all day.

The Santa costume was his way of putting a shield between himself and the islanders' judgmental gazes, not something to bring everyone closer together. No one had been blunt enough to say anything, and any condolences for his loss had been whispered out of earshot of Audrey, but he was sure he could sense their judgement in the air. Well-deserved judgement.

He made a mental note not to ask Audrey for a full psychological assessment unless he wanted a hard, very uncomfortable look in the mirror. He also reminded himself to try not to push her buttons with such regularity. There was obviously a lot more going on beneath the calm, professional surface Audrey had let their patients see. Something he instinctively felt he could relate to if they were to open up to one another. Which, all things considered, was unlikely.

'Please,' he said, putting out a hand. 'Accept my apology. I'm used to the rough and tumble of an inner-city emergency department. There's not much time for manners there. How about we rewind and work on things from… I don't know…? How about hello? Would that work? Give each other a clean slate and start over?'

'I've got a better idea,' Audrey sniped, instead of laughing and taking his hand as he'd hoped. 'Why don't we keep this professional relationship precisely that.'

'What? Professional?'

She pinned on a smile that definitely didn't hit her eyes. 'Top of the class, were you?'

'Not at charm school.'

The corners of her mouth twitched and then, even though he could see she was trying not to, she finally smiled. A hit of pride sent his heart banging against his ribcage. Teasing a genuine smile out of her made him feel like a medal winner. Maybe that was where he'd gone wrong. Too much time trying to keep his emotions at bay when in actual fact a bit of time in the emotional trenches made moments like this much more rewarding.

A few minutes later, with a more companionable air between them, they pulled up to the surgery.

'Let's get you to your accommodation, shall we?' he said.

Audrey got of the car and stretched. 'I could definitely do with a hot shower and a nice warm bed.'

'I'm afraid that won't be possible.'

They both turned at the sound of a male voice.

'Dr Anstruther?' Cooper squinted against the bright security light that popped on as a figure came down the alleyway alongside the high street surgery.

'Hello, there, Coop.' Dr Anstruther emerged onto the street. 'Audrey.'

Cooper was sorry to see the much-respected doctor looking very much his seventy-odd years this evening. 'What's going on? Is everything all right?' he asked, and beckoned to Audrey to join them.

The silver-haired doctor gave Cooper a clap on the shoulder, then put out a hand to shake Audrey's. 'Finlay Anstruther, dearie. I know we met earlier, but we were both so rushed it wasn't much of a greeting. And I'm afraid you'll not be getting much of one now.'

'Why?' Cooper asked when Audrey failed to.

'Erm, well…' His eyes travelled up to the flat above the surgery, where locum doctors and nurses stayed.

Cooper's stomach dropped. 'Has something happened?'

Finlay Anstruther winced. 'Aye. Boiler's gone. Water pipes burst after that freeze we had the other day, I'm guessing. I've not been up there for a few days, but when my Emily went in to give the place a wee clean a couple of hours back—disaster. I was trying to fix it myself, but then I saw the staining on the ceiling of my office down in the surgery—'

He made a despairing noise. One that didn't speak well for the safety of working in the surgery.

'Why didn't you call any of the lads?'

By 'lads', Cooper meant the men he'd been born and raised with, right here on this island. Men taught their trade by their fathers as they'd been taught by their fathers before them. Unlike Cooper who, if he'd followed his own father's path, would be leaving two orphaned children behind about now.

Finlay tugged a hand through his shock of white hair. 'Son, it's not good. Not good at all.'

'The flat or the surgery?' Cooper asked.

'Both.'

'Ah…' This was awkward. 'Anything we can do about it tonight?' He fastidiously avoided Audrey's pained expression while he waited for Finlay's inevitable answer.

'No, not really, son. Audrey, I'm ever so sorry. Everyone's up at the Nativity rehearsal, and it's not as if the flat'll be habitable any time today or…'

The fact he'd left the sentence unfinished spoke to just how bad the burst pipe problem actually was.

* * *

Audrey looked between the pair of them as if she were watching a game point rally at Wimbledon, and then, unexpectedly, she laughed. 'It looks like Baby Jesus and I share a similar housing problem. But surely there's a B&B I can stay in, or a hotel? There's no need to worry about me.'

Cooper and the veteran GP exchanged a charged look. 'Not this time of year, darlin',' Finlay offered, then repeated his apologies.

He promised to speak to all the relevant tradesmen tonight, to see what could be done, but in the meantime... He and his wife had put their house on the market, and had most of their things in storage in advance of his retirement, so there wasn't a room for her there...

Cooper had half tuned out as his brain was heading down a very narrow tunnel. He'd known Finlay was going to hang up his hat, but now that he was talking about actually having put things in storage and literally preparing to up stakes it was like a bucket of icy cold North Sea water on his face.

There was a job for life if he wanted it, here on Bourtree Castle. *Was* this what he wanted? To stay here for ever? To have the folk of Bourtree growing accustomed to him dressing as

Santa as he did his rounds each Christmas? As the Easter bunny in spring?

Or, to really boil it down to its purest essence, did he want the people of Bourtree to think of him as a doctor they could rely on to stay?

When he tuned back in Finlay was rattling off the number of folk who had come back from the mainland to stay with family, drop presents off in case the ferries were grounded owing to bad weather, make Christmas cakes with grans, bird houses with grandads… The list seemed to go on for ever.

Cooper stopped the flow of excuses in the only way he knew how. 'She can stay with me, Finlay.'

It was a step closer towards 'getting to know you' than he would've preferred, but he was hardly going to leave Audrey here on the High Street with her fingers crossed that someone would offer her a room for the night.

'Um…"she" is right here,' Audrey said, about an octave higher than she normally spoke, air quotes hanging in the wintry air. 'And "she" will not be staying with you. Now, Finlay, are you sure there's—?'

'There's nowhere else, dearie,' Finlay said sorrowfully. 'Not this time of year. We're such a small population at the best of times, what with folk seeking their fortunes elsewhere.' His

eyes flicked briefly to Cooper's, but there was
no malice in his words, just acceptance. 'Cooper's offer is a good one. I'd take it. Now, if
you two'll excuse me, Emily's going to have my
head if I don't get down the church hall sharpish. Coop, shall we meet up at the usual time
to discuss what to do about the surgery? The
reception area's fine—it's my room that's the
potential problem.'

'Fine. Put it out of your head for tonight. As
you say, it'll be a problem solved tomorrow.
Now...' Cooper turned his attention to Audrey
as Finlay headed off towards the church. 'Don't
look so worried. It's not a smelly bachelor pad.
It's more...'

He saw her eyes narrow suspiciously as he
sought the perfect word to describe his grandmother's house.

'More what?'

'You'll see,' he said, tossing in a smile to reas-
sure her that it wasn't *bad*...it was just...well...
she'd see.

'Gosh. It's...wow...um... Your grandmother's
sense of style is... I've never seen anything like
it.'

Cooper smiled at Audrey's understated response to his grandmother's house. He probably should've warned her. Or given her a pair

of sunglasses before he flicked on the overhead lights.

Opening the front door each night was such a bittersweet experience it was strangely helpful, having Audrey here. Most of the girlfriends he'd had would've smirked and made snarky comments about the doilies and the abundance of crocheted bric-a-brac. It was partly why he'd never brought anyone to Bourtree. No chance he'd subject his gran to their sneers.

But Audrey was different. She seemed delighted by it. Though she hadn't found the perfect words to describe it, he got the sense that she felt as though she'd been allowed to see something special. And, as nearly everything in here had been made by his grandmother, it was.

He took off his coat and made a show of shaking the down into submission as he watched Audrey absorb just how much his grandmother had loved using the woollen mill's bin-ends, whether or not they matched. Her ethos had been the brighter the better. Every day needed a bit of sunshine, according to her, and for nine months of the year in Bourtree? You weren't going to get it from the sky.

Audrey took a step into the lounge and ran her hand along the knitted—or crocheted?—blanket that was draped over the back of the tartan-patterned sofa. 'Did she make *all* of this?'

She sounded impressed.

'Sure did.' It was good to be able to feel a puff of pride about her, the woman who'd raised him when his mum and dad had proved utterly inept at parenting.

He scanned the room along with Audrey. His gran had made each and every blanket, cushion cover, tatted picture frame. To be honest, she'd taken her love of household needlework to an entirely different level. He'd was quite certain every bairn on the island had been swaddled in one of his gran's blankets at one juncture or another. And then, of course, there were the doilies. Dozens of the things. On every arm-rest…under every china figure. The figures were women, mostly in period dress, their china skirts caught in an invisible breeze as their bonnets dangled from their fingers.

'No Christmas tree?' asked Audrey.

'Nope,' Cooper said, a bit too briskly for someone wearing a Santa suit. 'Believe it or not, I'm not usually in the habit of decorating for Christmas.'

'But it isn't about you, is it? Shouldn't it be about what your grandmother's routine is—?'

'Was,' he quietly corrected, rawly aware of how wrong it felt to describe someone as full of life as his gran in the past tense.

Audrey turned and touched his arm. 'Oh,

Cooper, I'm so sorry. I suppose I should've put two and two together, but we were so busy—'

'Bickering?' Cooper finished for her.

'No, not bickering.' Audrey looked around the small lounge again, as if hoping to find the right word. 'We were…figuring one another out. And please do accept my condolences about your grandmother. Was it recent?'

'Just over a week back,' he said, a harsh sting of emotion scraping his throat as he fought against admitting that he should've been here and hadn't been. He *could've* been here. He'd done ten days on the trot at the hospital and had been owed a few days off. Weeks, really. But had he taken them?

Of course not.

Winter was always busy in the A&E and, as usual, there had been no one for him to go home to, so he'd signed up for a double shift after a quick call to his gran, to remind her to make sure there was more lemon and honey than whisky in her hot toddy. As if she'd needed reminding. She knew what too much booze did to a person.

'It must be tough, being here with all these memories.' His eyes snapped to Audrey's. Was she telling him something?

'Is that what you're doing?' he asked. 'Dodging memories?'

Any warmth that had bloomed between them vanished. 'No,' she said crisply. 'I prefer to focus on making new ones.'

So that was a yes, then.

He thought of the way her thumb kept creeping towards her bare ring finger. Not that he'd been wondering about her availability. Much…

'If you don't mind, Cooper, I'd like to see my room. It's been a long day.'

'Of course. Sorry.'

He did the short tour from the centre of the house, pointing out where everything was. Lounge, kitchen, dining room… His room upstairs. His gran's at the far end of the corridor, leading out to the back garden, the dining room opposite it.

'This looks like it was her knitting room rather than her dining room,' Audrey commented.

Cooper resisted taking the statement as a barb. He and his gran hadn't sat down for a proper meal in the dining room in well over a decade. On the rare occasions when he'd come home he'd insisted on taking her out to the Puffin. A meagre thanks for all she'd sacrificed to keep him on the straight and narrow.

The money he would give now to have one more meal with her the way they'd used to…

kitting out the table as if the Queen herself were coming for tea.

'*Why not?*' his gran had used to quip as she pulled out a crystal tumbler for his soft drink. '*You never know which moment will be your last, so best to make all of them special.*'

He'd used to think that comment had been about his parents. He supposed the difference was that theirs had been an accident waiting to happen with the way they drank. His gran's death had been preventable, and it was on him that it hadn't been prevented.

He showed Audrey into his sister's old room. It was kitted out in soft yellow and cream colours. Apart from a picture of the two of them, from when they were kids, it could easily have been a room in any B&B. His grandmother's room had the nicer view, but it was far too soon to turn it into anything other than a place to reflect on the ways he could improve himself.

'Oh, it's much more…um…neutral in here,' Audrey said.

Cooper shrugged. 'My sister always preferred to blend in.'

Audrey cocked her head to the side, interested. 'I didn't know you had a sister.'

Cooper shrugged. 'She's a few years older than me and she moved to New Zealand years back.' They'd both been 'surprises' to his parents. Unwelcome ones.

'Did she come back for the funeral?'

No. She hadn't. Like him, she'd found growing up as a child of the island's two lushes complicated. She had a family of her own now. A happy life. Kept herself to herself. As if he, too, was part of her complicated history. *Fight or flight*. They'd both chosen the latter. Unfortunately in different directions.

'Long trip.'

'I suppose it is,' she said, with a hit of compassion warming those dark eyes of hers.

He waited for the inevitable follow-up comment. Lord knew he'd received enough of them as he'd shaken everyone's hand at the end of Gertie's funeral. *'Not good enough for your sister, are we? Your gran gave you two bairns everything she had. The least Shona could've done was fly up to pay her respects.'*

Cooper had pointed out that the biggest floral tribute had been from his sister, but absence didn't make the heart grow fonder in the islanders' eyes. It chipped away at the loyalty they believed you owed them.

He pointed at the fireplace at the far end of the room. 'There is central heating, but it's not brilliant. If you like, you can light the fire.'

'Oh, I've never had a fire in my bedroom before.' Audrey's eyes glittered with excitement.

'Grand. If the weather drops, as it's meant to, we'll need all the wood fires going. But don't worry—you won't have to blast your way through the wood pile or anything.'

'Why?'

Because chopping wood had been about the only way he'd kept his sanity over the past fortnight. As if physically pounding out his sorrows would eventually bring him peace.

'That's my job.'

Audrey instantly stood up straighter, irritation replacing the glee of having her own wood fire. 'I suppose you think I can't chop wood because I'm a girl?'

'I wouldn't dare suggest such a thing,' Cooper said, the corners of his mouth twitching ever so slightly.

Oh, he wanted to annoy her, did he? *Job done, pal.* That showed her what softening her stiff resolve to dislike him would do. Catch her out at the first opportunity. Well, she wasn't having Cooper suffer from the delusion that she was a poor helpless girl unable to fend for herself for a moment longer.

'I bet you think I'd freeze to death by the end of the week if left to my own devices.' She balled her hands into fists, waiting for him to confirm her comment.

Rafael would certainly have said as much. What she'd initially seen as gentlemanly behaviour, she was now beginning to see for what it was: good old-fashioned sexism. She'd been in charge of the fluffier things in their relationship, like their wedding. Rafael had been in charge of everything else.

It had been more subtle than that, of course. But the fact she'd been so blind to the effortless shift her life had taken back to the nineteen-fifties made her want to show hindsight exactly how firm a grip she had on her future.

If Cooper wanted to wear the 'Me Man, You Woman' mantel he'd have a fight on his hands. Even if she didn't have the remotest clue how to chop wood… Surely she could take a stab at it? It wasn't brain surgery. In the same way that changing a patient's dressing required a deft touch, she suspected wood-chopping had its own art.

An art she might be terrible at. *Oh, crumbs.* Why had she started an argument she didn't know if she could win?

The hint of humour had disappeared from Cooper's features and been replaced by earnest entreaty. 'I'd never suggest you couldn't do something because you're a woman. And not just because my grandmother's ghost would give short shrift to that.'

Audrey tried to imagine a gran ghost appearing and chasing Cooper out of the house. She smiled.

'What?' he asked warily, as if he, too, could see the image.

'I don't have the slightest idea how to chop wood,' she admitted reluctantly.

'Oh?'

He looked surprised, but not shocked. Nor did he look disappointed. It struck her how conditioned she'd become to holding her breath whenever she'd admitted something to Rafael—something she didn't know how to do. Had she really wanted to be a part of such a marriage? A lifetime of feeling anxious about being herself?

Cooper leant against the doorframe. 'Want me to teach you?'

Wow. That fell into the realm of 'not remotely expected'. 'Yes!'

'Is that a real yes, or a yes just to prove a point?'

There wasn't any attitude accompanying his question. It was just a question—plain and simple.

'I think I'd like to learn how to chop wood,' Audrey said.

'We can do some next time we hit a bit of

daylight, if you like,' he said, flicking his thumb towards what she imagined was the back garden.

'Sure. Sounds good.'

They shared a smile that lit a small flame of hope in her. Not just for herself, but for her working relationship with Cooper. He may have some far-out ideas about seasonal 'uniforms', and he ping-ponged from grumpy to genuinely caring at the drop of a hat, but maybe this interchange was a sign they wouldn't spend the next five weeks bickering after all.

A swirl of something she didn't want to acknowledge whirled round her belly, teasing at areas she'd thought would never show signs of life again.

Interesting.

And not a little bit scary.

Cooper put his hand out and gave hers a solid shake. 'I'm looking forward to you taking over that part of the household workload.'

There was a twinkle in his eye as he said it, and a shot of electricity running up her arm as his hand shifted away from hers just a little more slowly than in your average handshake. As if he'd felt the same spray of energy running between them.

He cleared his throat and abruptly pushed himself up and away from the doorframe, giving his hands a brisk rub. 'Right, then, lassie. I know it seems early, but I'm away off to my bed. Are you hungry or anything?'

She shook her head. 'Those fish and chips were amazing. And huge.'

'Best in Scotland,' he said, a charming hint of pride ribboning round the statement. His eyes met hers, then flicked away. 'Right, so… Can I get you a tea or a hot chocolate for a nightcap?'

She shook her head. She didn't want to put him to any more trouble than she already had. 'I'm fine. A hot shower and bed will do me just fine.'

'Right you are, then.' He tipped an invisible cap and bade her goodnight.

She sat down on the bed, enjoying a little bounce when she discovered it was covered in inviting layers of handstitched quilts. She wished she could've met Cooper's gran. She must never have had an idle moment. Or been short of a lesson to share.

Her own childhood had been lovely, but a little bit lonely. It had pretty much just been her and her dad. He'd done the best he could to keep her happy and engaged, but she'd always envied other children who came from huge extended families, and had genuinely been looking forward to starting a family of her own with Rafael.

Which did beg the question... Had it been the family she'd wanted rather than the man? Perhaps she'd forgiven him all his controlling quirks because she'd had her eyes on a different prize. Children to laugh and play with. A family life that she herself had never had.

Whatever... That had been then, and a family was so off her radar right now it wasn't worth the energy even to think about it. She was a blank slate, waiting to discover what her real goals and dreams were.

So she'd lost a lying, cheating fiancé? There were worse things in life. Like losing a dearly loved grandmother. Seeing how Cooper was struggling with his emotions in the wake of losing Gertie...it touched her.

She looked round the room again and smiled. If, beneath the gruff exterior and the Santa suit, Cooper was anything like his gran, she was pretty sure there was a heart of gold buried beneath that red jacket of his.

CHAPTER FOUR

'IT'S NOT LOOKING GOOD, is it?'

Audrey, Finlay and Cooper all looked up at the large hole in the surgery's main examination room ceiling while Cooper aimed his heavy-duty torch around the area.

'Looks like a nice kitchen,' Audrey said dryly.

'Oh, it is,' Finlay agreed, a bit more earnestly than he should have considering there was a metre-wide sinkhole in the centre of it. 'Very.'

'Shall we get everything you need out of here and into the spare room, Finlay?'

Audrey was almost grateful to have someone else's problems to worry about. Almost because this particular problem meant she'd be staying with Cooper for the foreseeable future. If he'd have her.

She got the impression he was more the lone wolf type than a happy-to-have-a-housemate kind of guy. And also, she'd kind of accidentally imagined him getting undressed and climbing into bed last night, and that was an imaginary picture she hadn't been able to un-see. In a good way. A too good for words type of way. Which, of course, was strictly forbidden.

Cooper, who clearly hadn't thought about *her* getting undressed, was thinking far more practically. 'I think we should get everything we need and take it to another *building*.'

Audrey scanned the scene again. He was right. It looked as though a wrecking ball had dropped through the ceiling.

'C'mon, you lot.' Cooper abruptly flew into action. 'I'm pretty sure I saw some spare boxes back in the storeroom. I'll call the church. Finlay, can you ring whoever's on reception today and have them meet us there? We'll set up in the hall, like you did before when the blood drive folk came over.'

'You remember that?' Finlay asked.

'Aye,' Cooper said tightly, his features retracting in a micro-flinch.

He clearly remembered, but, Audrey amended, he didn't like being reminded that there was a lot he *hadn't* been around for.

Finlay gave Cooper's shoulder a pat. 'Nice thinking, son.'

Cooper's jaw relaxed, as if being called 'son' and treated as one of the island's own was a salve to whatever was troubling him.

She'd not yet had the courage to ask, but she was guessing things with his parents hadn't been that brilliant. Or maybe it was something with his grandmother…

'Are you happy to help with the packing up?' Cooper asked, when he noticed her staring at him a bit too intensely.

'Absolutely.' She held out her hand for a box, hoping he hadn't noticed her cheeks colouring.

Staring at Cooper, with all that tangled dark hair, those bright blue eyes, and much more than a hint of a five o'clock shadow, was a bit too easy. A bit too pleasurable.

Funny, considering she'd thought she'd never get lost in another man's beauty after— *Enough.* She needed to draw a line under that entire humiliating chapter. She lost three months of her life and a sizeable chunk of her dignity to that man, so onwards and upwards. It was the only way to move on.

As they began to pick up and dust off the essential things they needed, Audrey felt herself overcome with an unfamiliar sense of lightness. As if she'd been sprinkled with some sort of fairy dust.

Something about this disaster was striking her as… Well, not *funny*, exactly—because it was clearly an expensive problem, and the wrong time of year to have it, and it would definitely mean she'd be spending the rest of her stay at Cooper's gran's unless the Bourtree tradesmen were as efficient as Santa's elves—but she'd thought her entire life had fallen apart four days ago. Now she had been literally shown that all kinds of things could very easily go from bad to worse…and worse seemed survivable. Meaning she had more strength of character than she had given herself credit for.

She would survive this break-up. And the heartbreak, such as it was. And, more to the point, the shame.

She might not have shed her last tear, and would very likely never enjoy Christmas again, but that was something she was prepared to live with. Particularly when the clouds had cleared just enough for her to begin to appreciate the little things so much more than she had.

Like hot chocolate.

She grinned at the memory.

Last night, while she'd been in the shower, Cooper had made her a mug of hot chocolate despite the fact she'd said she didn't want to put him to the trouble. He'd slipped it onto her bedside table with a note and an alarm clock set for this morning.

It had been a kind gesture. One that had made her feel more welcome than she'd ever imagined feeling here. She'd gone on to sleep like a baby under all those dreamy quilts, and in the morning had woken up feeling cared for and protected in a way she hadn't felt since her father had died.

Family. That was what it had felt like. Being cared for by someone who understood the importance of being part of something bigger than yourself.

'You all right, Audrey?'

She looked up to see Cooper staring at her oddly. Somewhere amid his packing efforts he'd swirled a thick strand of silver tinsel round his neck. It gave him an air of carefree joy, whilst everything else about him was solid, focused male energy.

That increasingly familiar spray of heat blossomed in her belly as their eyes met and held. She wasn't about to tell him she was having an epiphany that a mug of hot chocolate could prove that there was still good in the world, so she gave him a neutral smile and carried on working, thinking that maybe—just maybe— she might have a tiny bit of room in her heart for Christmas after all.

An hour later they'd relocated to the pleasant church hall. It was a large, wood-floored, stone-walled room that could easily be divided into four smaller rooms with the portable partitions the church used for Sunday school and the like. There were also many boxes overflowing with animal costumes marked NATIVITY! DO NOT TOUCH!

By the time they'd set up, had a thorough run through the patient roster with Dr Anstruther and gone out to start their rounds, the sun still hadn't risen. But the Christmas lights twinkled away, strung as they were across the High Street and all the way up to the castle ruins, and, of course, so did the enormous Christmas tree. Quite a few lights were appearing in the High Street shops, too, indicating that the island of Bourtree was coming to life.

Cooper's phone started ringing just as they climbed into the big medical four-by-four. From what Audrey could glean, a hysterical mother had reached her wits' end with her teenager, who was refusing to go to school. Again.

Cooper spoke to her in his reassuringly steady brogue. 'Right, that's fine, Helen. We'll be over just as soon as we've made one other call on the way. No, no. It won't take long. You'll get to work on time, so stay where you are. Audrey and I— Audrey's the locum district nurse, remember? Noreen's off to Australia to see her grandbaby.'

There was a pause while Cooper listened.

'Yes. She's exactly the sort of person you'd want to talk with Cayley, okay? Listen. Put the kettle on. Make yourself a cuppa and we'll be there soon. Audrey and I will help you through, okay?'

Wow… Rafael had always made Audrey feel insecure about her choice to be a district nurse—to the point where she'd actually changed jobs. Cooper made her feel she was at the top of her game. It was an incredible feeling. Having someone who barely knew her honour the professional choice she'd always known deep in her heart was the right one for her.

'Thanks for that,' she said, before she could stop herself.

'What?'

'Speaking highly of me. Professionally, I mean.'

His brows arrowed towards his nose. 'Why wouldn't I? You're great at what you do.'

'It's just that—'

She stopped herself. Telling him that she'd allowed her fiancé to belittle her professionally was a bit too raw a confession right now.

'I jumped down your throat yesterday and…well, it's nice to know you noticed me. Because—I mean—you're really good at *your* job, and it means a lot to know that you think I'm good. I mean workwise… Obviously.' Heat began to creep into her cheeks. 'I think I'll just stop talking now.'

How embarrassing. She might as well have said, *I fancy you, but I don't want to, plus it means more than I can say that you think I'm good at my job.*

His look intensified for a moment, and then, as if he'd come to a conclusion, he looked away and turned the key in the ignition.

A few awkward moments later Audrey noticed something. 'No Santa outfit today?'

He flashed her one of those enigmatic smiles of his and gave the tinsel around his neck a flick. After he'd pulled the car out onto the main road, he dug in his pocket and pulled out the Santa hat. 'I thought I'd give Christmas more like just a nod today. Save my cool threads for the proper lead-up.'

Audrey swallowed back a comment about him changing his tune rather quickly, because the truth was that somewhere beneath that smile of his was a man grieving for his grandmother. A woman he clearly missed with all his heart. To be honest, Audrey was beginning to think the whole costume thing had been more to cheer him up than the patients they were seeing.

'I hope I didn't put you off,' Audrey said. 'I know I was pretty grumpy about the elf costume.'

She hadn't meant to be a party pooper... It was just that yesterday she'd been feeling emotionally bruised and vulnerable. Funny how fewer than twenty-four hours on this island had given her some much-needed space to breathe. Space, she was beginning to realise, Rafael had never given her.

'You weren't grumpy,' he said amiably, turning the car onto the coastal road that circumnavigated the island. Then, 'Maybe a little...'

'I'm sorry,' she said, more heartfelt than before. 'It really wasn't anything personal.' Not personal to him, anyway.

'No bother,' he said distractedly.

He pulled the car off onto a small, vaguely familiar lane and after a few minutes Audrey realised they were back at Jimmy Tarbot's.

They checked his insulin levels and gave him his injection, and Audrey was in the kitchen, making him a cup of tea before they left, when Cooper popped in, his medical gloves still on, and had a quick nosy in Jimmy's bin.

Rather than point out that it looked as if he was taking a page out of her book, she asked, 'What are you looking for?'

'Evidence,' he said, jiggling his eyebrows in a TV detective sort of way.

'Of what?'

'The tomato soup and salad he told me he had for his tea last night.' With a grim expression he lifted out an empty family-sized box of lasagne and an equally empty tub of double chocolate caramel ice cream. 'Not happy,' he said, peeling off his gloves and popping them into the disposal bag in his medical kit. 'He was also asking after my gran's biscuits.'

Audrey frowned. 'Is that a euphemism for something?'

Cooper cracked a smile and shook his head. 'No. My gran—Gertie—had this tradition of making endless amounts of biscuits around Christmas time. She'd bring them to folk, especially the ones who were housebound, so suffice it to say Jimmy's had a fair few through the years. She always made him a special batch—low sugar, or something like that.' He gave his jaw a scrub. 'She'd know what to do to get Jimmy out and about. Better than giving him a lecture and rooting about in his bin, anyway.'

Something squeezed tight in Audrey's chest. Cooper looked genuinely invested in Jimmy's welfare. As if he had to pick up where his grandmother had left off and pour kindness into a community that sometimes struggled to stay afloat.

Cooper abruptly clapped his hands together, then gave Audrey a cheeky grin. 'I might have an idea.'

Cooper headed back into the lounge, where Jimmy seemed to reside permanently on the sofa. The duvet stuffed behind it suggested he might even sleep there.

'Hey, Jim!'

Audrey didn't actively earwig, but she caught a few things. Something about getting his next injection down at the church. And if Jimmy needed someone to come here and help him to get up and out of the house that'd be fine.

She turned on the tap to wash her hands and missed the end.

Cooper came back in and shouldered the medical run-bag. 'All right?'

'Yes, indeed.' They left and went to the car. 'So,' she asked, 'are we picking up Jimmy later?'

Cooper nodded, his eyes on the rear-view mirror as he reversed the car out onto the road. 'Aye. I think he's becoming a bit too reclusive for his own good.'

'And you think a trip to the church hall would help?'

'I think knowing the islanders don't mean any harm by still calling him Big Jim would do him good.' He shot her a quick smile. 'And I've got an idea.'

'Plan to share?'

'No.' He shook his head, a mischievous twinkle lighting up his eyes as he said, 'Not just yet.'

Audrey laughed. 'Okay, mystery man. Who's next?'

Ten minutes later, as they stood in the hall of their next patient's home, the light mood they'd been enjoying in the car had evaporated. Cayley, Helen's thirteen-year-old daughter, was refusing for the third day in a row to go to school, and this time wasn't even bothering to make up a fake illness. That was the part that had her mother worried.

It wasn't the kind of call they'd normally make as part of rounds, but Audrey had seen, when Cooper had taken Helen's call that morning there had been something about it that had made him say yes instantly.

'I simply don't know what to do.' Helen twirled her hair into a swift French twist, though it was still wet from the shower. 'She won't get out of bed. Keeps crying and saying she won't go to school again. Ever. She's only thirteen! That's no way to spend a childhood.'

Cooper gave Audrey a look, then returned his focus to Helen. 'I'm happy to talk to her, but if it's a sensitive issue…you know…' He swallowed uncomfortably.

Audrey was pretty sure where he was going with this, and found it a little bit adorable that a hardened A&E doctor should have trouble alluding to feminine matters. Maybe it was the fact he'd gone to school with Helen that did it? Who knew? He was a hard one to read, Cooper.

'Maybe she wants to talk about female issues?' Audrey gently finished for him.

'Which would be a talk much better had with you, Audrey.'

Cooper gave her a quick nod that managed to speak volumes. He wasn't feeling uncomfortable about 'female issues'. He was simply being considerate of his patient, and he was letting her take the lead. This would, after all, be the kind of call she'd be doing on her own in a week's time, unless the situation warranted two people.

Which begged the question…what would Cooper be doing? Leaving for Glasgow? That wouldn't be… Well, she didn't know what she felt about that, so it was probably best to go back to the 'live in the here and now' remit she'd assigned herself.

She forced herself to tune back into what he was saying.

'Audrey'll most likely suss it, but if she finds she needs prescriptions, or anything, I'll be happy to step in.'

Again, Audrey experienced a warm hit of gratitude. Cooper's belief in her abilities gave her a morale boost she hadn't known she needed. Sure, the whole rest of her life was a calamity, but her nursing skill—the one thing she'd al-

ways honoured about herself—was being given respect.

Why had being a district nurse never been good enough for her ex…? *Pfft.* Another question for another time.

'Will I go in with you?' the worried mum asked.

'Absolutely,' Audrey said, but then, after a second, thought it best to ask, 'Or do you think there's anything she'd be nervous about saying in front of you?'

'Not at all,' Helen said. 'That's why I'm so worried. Cayley and I have always been close. We've never kept secrets from one another.'

'Then let's go and find out what this is about,' Audrey said, giving her a reassuring smile.

Helen put a hand on her arm before they headed up to the bedroom. 'You should probably know that her father and I are no longer together. Not for a few months now.'

'Okay.'

Helen's grip tightened on Audrey's arm and her eyes darted towards Cooper. 'Brian, my ex, was often away on the oil rigs, and suffice it to say he played away as well. I've tried to keep the gossip away from Cayley, but it's a small island, so…'

She didn't need to finish the sentence. Audrey had been working in a small hospital when her

wedding plans had imploded, and the last thing she'd wanted to do was face the other nurses when news had spread like wildfire that the wedding was off.

'Right you are. Well, let's go in and have a chat, shall we?'

Keeping the memories at bay was proving difficult, so Cooper did what he imagined Audrey would do. Popped the kettle on.

He stared out of Helen's kitchen window. She lived a couple of streets back from Bourtree High Street in a small but cosy terraced house. Two up, two down. A brightly painted front door. A small garden where she could peg out the laundry in the summer and keep a wood pile in the winter.

For as long as he could remember, Bourtree Castle folk had always liked to say they never needed nowt beyond a home like this to have a nice life. His parents hadn't been able to hold on even to that. Their bill down at the pub had always kept the dream of a home of their own out of reach. So they'd all crammed into his gran's house.

And when they'd hit that sharp bend down at the far end of the island and forgotten to turn the car along with it…well…

He turned as he heard Cayley's muted voice

through the ceiling, pitching and peaking as she presumably explained why she wouldn't leave her room. Whatever she was going through, it was hitting her hard.

Cooper had three mugs of sweet tea ready to go by the time the women came out. Audrey had her arm around Helen's shoulders, and she gave her a proper, reassuring hug before turning her around to accept the mug Cooper held out for her.

'Everything okay?' he asked, when no one said anything.

Audrey and Helen exchanged a quick look. Then through an unspoken agreement Audrey began to explain. 'The children at school have been picking on her.'

An acrid taste rose in Cooper's throat. Kids could be great, but they could also be bloody cruel. 'What about?'

'She has a crush on a lad in the class above her and he already has a girlfriend.'

Cooper looked between the pair of them. 'Kids get crushes on people who aren't available all the time. Why give Cayley a hard time about it?'

'The girlfriend—' Audrey began, then backtracked. 'Bear in mind we're talking about twelve and thirteen-year-olds here—raging hormones, first loves—'

'That early?' Cooper asked before he could stop himself.

He'd been so busy having fights behind the bike shed with the bullies who'd taunted him about his parents he'd not had time to worry about falling in love. To be honest, he wasn't entirely sure he'd ever made the time.

Yes, he'd had girlfriends. Here and in Glasgow. But he was pretty sure something all his exes would agree on if—God forbid—they ever got together and had a chinwag about him, was the fact that he'd never invested enough time in any of them. He'd cared about them— of course. But had he ever made a one hundred percent emotional investment? Nope. Getting too close to people meant disappointing them in the end. That or discovering they never wanted you in the first place.

Loving someone with all his heart only led to pain. His grandmother being the latest case in point.

'Whether or not it's true love isn't the point,' Audrey said, with a bit more bite than he would've expected.

'Okay. So, what *is* the point?'

'The bullying. They're saying she's been cheating with the boy when she hasn't. And they're saying she's—' Audrey threw an apol-

ogetic look in Helen's direction. 'They're saying she's her father's daughter.'

Ah. The penny dropped. 'They're bullying her about something she has no power over?'

Audrey nodded, her brow crinkling as their eyes met. His heart strained against his ribcage as he looked into her eyes. She wasn't looking *at* him. She was looking directly *into* him. Into everything that had made him the man he was today—including the young Coop emerging from behind the bike sheds, wiping away the blood before the teachers saw. And the boy rearranging his features to look as though he didn't have a care in the world when all he wanted was parents who had his corner. Who loved him.

'So, what are your thoughts?' he asked, his voice a bit rougher than usual.

Audrey lowered her voice after a quick look back towards the stairwell. 'I think she could probably do with a week or so off school. It's been going on for some time, and she's become very anxious. She's lost weight...isn't sleeping well. It'd be best to do something before she's properly unwell—'

Helen interjected. 'I know I should've kept a closer eye on her, but I've had to do double shifts to get some money in for Christmas, since we're not getting any from her father.'

'What?' Cooper only just managed to contain

a blast of rage. 'Brian isn't paying his maintenance costs?'

Helen shook her head. 'We've not even got through the divorce proceedings yet. I'm so behind on everything, I—' Her face screwed up tight and the tears began to flow. 'I've been trying so hard not to have anything else in Cayley's life change, but with the mortgage and the bills and Christmas coming, I guess I've let it all get on top of me.'

'Brian should be sending you money whether or not a judge has decreed it,' Cooper said. Unable to stop himself, he barrelled on. 'A man has a child—he needs to accept responsibility. Not leave someone else to sort out the pain at being rejected.'

The words were out before he could stop them. So much for keeping his cards close to his chest.

Both women fell into a thoughtful silence.

Damn.

It wasn't like him to put a knife to his own chest and bare all. He yanked the tinsel from around his neck and stuffed it in his pocket. 'Apologies, ladies. Topic's a bit too close to the bone.'

'I know, Coop,' Helen said gently, throwing a quick glance in Audrey's direction before con-

tinuing, 'And we're all so proud of you. The man you've become despite everything.'

Again he felt that flare of fury. And this time it was coupled with the heat of Audrey's inquisitive gaze.

Terrific. Now there was yet another person added to the list of people who would judge him because of his past. His parents' reputation as the island's drunks would always be a yoke round his neck. It was why he'd left. Why he'd found it hard to return despite how much he loved his gran.

That loyalty speech he'd given worked both ways. She'd sacrificed a lot for him. Raised two sets of children when she should've only had to raise one. It had been her turn to be looked after, but he'd found the memories too painful. Doubly so when he considered how badly trying to outrun them had panned out.

He shoved the thought into a dark corner.

'Are there any counselling services here on the island?' Audrey asked, tactfully turning things back to where their attention should be: on Cayley.

Cooper gave her a grateful nod. He could've done with someone like Audrey to talk with back in the day. Or a counsellor. Anyone to take the burden off his gran.

Her method had been to set him to a task. An

un-chopped wood pile being the most frequent chore. Or a job down at the Puffin, scrubbing pots. Loading boxes at the woollen mill. Burning off his rage had worked for him. Mostly. Talking probably would've taken care of the rest, but of all the things he and his gran hadn't done it was talk. As if acknowledging just how badly things had gone with his parents would have shattered them both.

He quickly flicked through the list of resources he kept on his phone. 'There's someone at the school. I'll give her a ring and see if she can pop over here in her lunch hour and have a chat. There's also a specialist who comes over once a fortnight, so long as the weather's all right for the ferry.'

'That sounds great,' said Helen. 'I just—I want to help her. Take away the pain. But—I feel like this is partly my fault. That there's something I must've done to drive Brian away, you know?' Helen wiped away a fresh wash of tears with a tissue Audrey handed her.

Helen's admission drove a stake into Cooper's heart. It had never once occurred to him that his grandmother might've been carrying the burden of guilt all those years. That the reason she'd never pushed him to come back was the sorrow she'd felt that her son had treated his children so badly.

It doubled the love he felt for her in an instant. Love he wished like hell he'd shared with her. More proof, if he needed any, that he wasn't fit to love anyone properly. Not with his broken bag of emotional tools.

'Hey, shush…' Audrey gave Helen a hug. 'You're doing the best you can in a bad situation.'

Helen blew her nose again and did her best to put on a brave face. 'I'm really sorry, but I've got to get to work. The counselling sounds good…but once a fortnight doesn't sound all that brilliant. Do you think that's enough?'

'It's early days yet,' Audrey soothed. 'It sounds like the local counsellor is a good resource. If you add a talk or two with the specialist to that, you could probably avoid putting her on medication,' Audrey said.

Helen's eyes widened. 'Do you think she'll need that?'

Cooper shook his head when Audrey sent him a questioning look. 'I've not seen her, obviously. But I trust Audrey's judgement. If she's up for a wee chat with me now, I can do a quick exam to officially sign her off school.'

Helen made a frustrated noise in her throat. 'I hate to think of her missing all her classwork. I know she's struggling with maths as it is.'

'I can help her,' Cooper said.

Helen gave him a suspicious look. 'Aye, that's nice, Coop, but I'd really rather have someone who's…you know…going to stick around for a while. She's had so much change already.'

Cooper wanted to protest. Say his plan was to stay for good this time. But something stopped him. Something that felt an awful lot like the truth.

He wanted to stay here. Wanted to make up for all those weeks and months—years, really— he'd stayed away when he should've been here with his gran, giving her that loving payback she'd so very much deserved.

An angry, orphaned teenager had probably been the last thing she'd wanted. His parents had died just as she'd retired, and he, more than anyone, knew how much she'd wanted to travel the world. But she hadn't. She'd stayed right here in Bourtree to look after him. And then he'd buggered off to Glasgow to seek his own fortune.

He might not be able to help his grandmother any more, but he could help Cayley.

'I'll do it, Helen.'

Audrey looked up from the paperwork she'd been filling out as if something in his voice had caught her attention. His desire to make good on a promise, no doubt.

From the smile appearing on her lips, it

seemed she respected a man who made good
on his word. But before he could get off track,
wondering who or what had let Audrey down,
his phone buzzed. It was Dr Anstruther, sending along the details for another house call to
tack onto their list.

'Okay. So that's settled. Shall I have a word
with Cayley to see how we stand?'

Audrey opened her mouth to say something,
then clamped it shut, waving away his questioning look. 'You go on.'

A few minutes later he was drawing his talk
with Cayley to a close. The poor girl was obviously stricken with an intense case of anxiety.

He'd seen far too many doctors write out prescriptions as a first response, but he hated to
put children on medication, preferring to see if
he could build a support system around them
instead. Obviously in extreme cases he'd do
whatever was necessary, but he could see little
glimmers of hope for Cayley, and felt reassured
that being around supportive people might help
her.

His secondary role as maths tutor would be
a handy way of ensuring she was getting on all
right. And the fact she'd already opened up to
Audrey was a good sign. Even if she hadn't said
more than a few words, sometimes giving the

body's nervous system a bit of a rest was the best way to make a change.

'So, you think you're up for talking to someone a couple of times a week?'

Cayley nodded shyly, her eyes not meeting his. 'Is Audrey free? Maybe she could talk with me instead of Miss MacIntyre or...?'

Cooper laughed. 'You mean instead of me?' Luckily, he didn't take this stuff personally.

Cayley nodded again, her brown eyes peeping up at him through her thick fringe. Bless. He didn't blame her. If he was having trouble the last person he'd want to talk to was—well... anyone, really. Saying that, he too could easily imagine sharing things he'd kept locked in his emotional black box with Audrey. Which was weird. Because if there was one thing he was not, it was a sharer. Maybe, just like Cayley, he needed someone in his life who would listen—and, more to the point, someone who wouldn't judge.

'Audrey's here for a few weeks, but I'm afraid she's going to be busy with her district nursing work.'

'And you?'

'I'll be around.' It was as close as he could come to a long-term commitment right now.

A silence fell between them.

Oh, hell.

'Look, Miss MacIntyre's free for a chat this afternoon if you like. And I'll be seeing you a couple times a week to go through your maths homework while you're off school. I'll also see about an appointment with the specialist counsellor who comes over from Glasgow. The main thing is we want you to know you've got a team of people around you. All here to listen.'

Cayley's mouth screwed up in the same tight moue her mother's had when she was about to cry.

'Hey, now, Cayley. Easy there, pet. I know things have been rough, but we're getting you help.'

The tears came. Desperation kicked in. He was used to lads straight in from bar brawls, not weeping tweens. Weeping tweens who were going through some remarkably familiar childhood trauma. He'd bashed through it with his fists and an axe. Cayley was too fragile to go that route. And, to be honest, it wasn't a route he'd recommend.

'Look. I'll have a word and see if Audrey'll pop in when she can, all right? She's just not a counsellor, that's all. I thought someone who's used to speaking to children who've been through what you have might be a bit more useful.'

'But Audrey *does* understand about broken

hearts!' she cried. 'Her fiancé cheated on her just like Dad cheated on Mum.'

Wait a minute. What?

Oh, hell. The poor woman. While the knowledge gave him little solace, it certainly gave him added insight. And a strange feeling of camaraderie.

So it wasn't just him who hit the road when the going got tough. He'd bundled all his sorrow and rage into a machine-like focus to become the best A&E doctor he could. Helping people and then disappearing out of their lives. Audrey was only just figuring out how to process the pain. Poor lass. It definitely explained why a London girl had appeared out here in the middle of nowhere just a few weeks before Christmas. It might also explain her aversion to Santa. Not that there was an obvious way to connect the dots on that one, but…

Cayley wove her fingers together under her chin. 'I was hoping she might be able to help me. You know…teach me how to take control of my own destiny like she did after her engagement broke up.'

'I see,' Cooper said, trying to appear as if the news wasn't brand-spanking-new to him.

Audrey had been *engaged*? As mad as it seemed, he already hated the guy. And that was without knowing a thing about him. Once he did he was pretty sure he'd dislike him even more. Audrey was a woman to love. To cherish.

'I'll have a word with her. See if perhaps the two of you can have a hot chocolate or something.'

Cayley's eyes brightened. 'Seriously? You'd do that?'

'I'll ask her, sure. But no promises. Okay?'

'Okay.' Cayley solemnly nodded. 'Thank you.'

'You're very welcome, young lady. I'll ring your mum later on today, but in the meantime you rest up and take care of yourself—all right?'

She gave him a grateful smile and nestled back under her duvet, her eyes already half closed as the comfort of knowing help was at hand eased her into much-needed sleep.

As he wrapped things up with Cayley's mum, Cooper had more questions than answers occupying his mind—and most of them were about Audrey.

CHAPTER FIVE

AUDREY CLIMBED DOWN from the big four-by-four, stretched and shivered. The heating system in the car was still faulty and it had been a long day. Rewarding, but long. She knew that instead of the patient roster being 'a bunch of geriatrics needing their bedding changed'—as her ex had liked to describe her patients—there was a huge variety of reasons patients were unable to get to a doctor.

What had struck her most was the disappointment from the patients they'd also seen yesterday that Cooper wasn't dressed up as Santa again. Maybe she should've dialled back her grumpiness. It wasn't as if everyone else needed to be miserable because she was. And…to be honest…now that she was away from her life in London, she was beginning to see how blinkered she had become.

Wedding plans. Getting herself on high-profile surgical rosters so she could impress Rafael.

Making sure she didn't embarrass Rafael at any of the seasonal soirées they'd been invited to…

There had been an awful lot of energy devoted to pleasing Rafael. Her father had often told her that loving someone meant celebrating the person you were, not changing who you were to fit someone else's plans. Why hadn't she remembered that when Rafael had opened that tell-tale blue box?

Cooper had been in an equally reflective mood in the car. Something told her his silence stemmed from what Helen had said about the islanders being proud of Cooper becoming the man he was 'despite everything'.

Despite what?

He definitely had issues with his father. That much was clear. He despised bullies—which spoke well of him as a man—and he honoured the responsibilities that came with being a parent. He hadn't really mentioned his mum. But he'd clearly adored his grandmother.

Audrey would've been better off falling in love with someone like him than Rafael.

Er… *What?*

Falling in love with *anyone* was strictly off-limits right now—especially Cooper. Work wasn't off-limits. She could think about that. And Cooper only professionally. *Obviously.*

Earlier in the afternoon Cooper had actually

managed to convince Jimmy Tarbot to leave his house and come to the church hall for his insulin check and injection. There, more to her surprise, Jimmy had been cornered by an earnest-looking man with some questions about lighting for the Nativity.

She'd caught a glance of complicity passing between Cooper and the man as Jimmy had launched into a detailed explanation about the inner workings of the lighting system. A shared smile at a job well done. When Cooper had caught her questioning look he'd muttered something about Jimmy being on the stage management team at school.

In the car, he'd withdrawn into the brooding silence he sometimes cloaked himself in when they weren't with patients. Now they were about to get something to eat at the Puffin Inn. Maybe she should just ask him.

Yeah, right. And then maybe she should pour her heart out to him about how she'd just been through the most confidence-crushing experience of her entire life. About as likely as her voluntarily jumping into the elf's costume still hanging in the back of the car.

'I've been thinking,' Cooper said as he came round to the front of the Jeep.

'Oh?' Audrey said warily. Hopefully mind-reading wasn't one of his skills.

'About Cayley.'

Ah. Good. She could talk about their patients all day if he wanted. She, too, had been worrying about the poor girl. 'Did you hear from the child psychologist over in Glasgow?'

He shook his head. 'Nah. It's crazy over there this time of year. I probably won't hear for a day or two unless I pull some strings.' He caught her gaze, then added, as if she was checking his professionalism, 'Which I might if she doesn't improve over the next couple of days. But I was thinking more along the lines of getting her out of the house while she's off school.'

Audrey rubbed her hands together and pointed towards the pub. Being somewhere warm to have this conversation was definitely going to help her brain work a bit better. 'I thought she had schoolwork to do?'

'She does,' Cooper said. 'But what kid do you know who can fill an entire day with schoolwork at home?'

Audrey threw him a smile. 'None.'

'Exactly.' He pulled open the door to the Puffin's entryway. The foyer was already filled with winter coats and a few pairs of work boots. 'I was thinking maybe we could get her down here.'

'What? The pub?'

He shook his head. 'No. Although having a

job probably wouldn't be a bad idea either. It'd give her a sense of pride. Of accomplishment.'

Audrey nodded, adding yet another square to the Cooper quilt. It sounded as though he'd once done the same thing.

'I was thinking more of getting her down to the church hall.'

'Why? So Dr Anstruther can keep an eye on her?'

Cooper threw a wave in the direction of the evergreen-swagged bar, where a man and a woman were busy pulling pints for a row of men in ferry uniforms. He called out to them that they'd be eating dinner and would get drinks in a minute.

'I was thinking more of getting her a job on the Nativity. The fact that Dr Anstruther would be there is a bonus,' he admitted. 'And a helpful precautionary measure. He's known her since she was a baby. Either way, I'm sure they could do with an extra pair of hands, seeing as half the island are needing costumes.'

Audrey laughed. 'If I didn't know better, I would think you have some sort of vested interest in the Nativity.'

Something dark flashed through his eyes. *Ouch.* Looked as if she was back on touchy territory. Best to let him fill in the blanks.

As they silently worked their way across the

thick wooden floor, worn with age, towards a table near the inglenook fireplace, Audrey noted the dip and then the rise of hushed murmurs as they passed the bar. A memory of the islanders taking bets on Cooper's staying power came back to her. Could that be what they were talking about? His lack of Santa suit could definitely sway things in the 'leave' direction.

Cooper strode on as if he'd heard and seen nothing.

The pub, clearly a good two or three hundred years old, managed to have a solid, spacious feeling about it. It was just over half full, and conversation, now that it had returned to normal, was buzzing, but not overloud. The mismatched chairs had sheepskin throws or wool blankets on them, and if Audrey wasn't mistaken she was pretty certain that the ferry men sitting at the bar were in their stockinged feet.

It felt as warm and welcoming as the church hall did. Apart, of course, from the whispering.

Cooper held a chair out for her as if he'd been doing it for years. Ridiculous, she knew, but she blushed. When her ex had done it, it had felt showy. As if he wanted the whole world to know what a gentleman he was, rather than being simply content to do something kind for his fiancée.

For Cooper, being considerate seemed second

nature. His grandmother? Or that heart of gold she suspected was lurking beneath the gruff exterior he was now sporting?

'We should have a word with the woman in charge of costumes,' Cooper said, pointing out the chalkboard menu on the wall as he did.

'What makes you think it's a woman?' Audrey teased, trying to lighten the atmosphere.

'It's always been a woman,' Cooper said, his eyes scanning the drinks menu he'd pulled out from between the salt and pepper shakers.

She bristled. How was she meant to know who was in charge of Nativity costumes on an island five hundred miles away from her home? Former home, anyway. Her indignation grew. Cooper was acting as if Audrey should know it was the natural order of things. Men on lights. Women on costumes.

Heart surgeons cheated. Nurses discovered their fiancés didn't really care if the wedding was on or off.

Unable to stop herself, she fuzzed her lips and rolled her eyes. 'Typical male.'

'Oh?' Cooper countered, a hint of a smile playing upon his lips. 'There's such a thing as a "typical male"? Who is this "typical" heterogametic, then?'

Audrey froze for a minute, then flopped back against the fluffy sheepskin on her chair.

It was a good question, actually. One to which she didn't have an instant answer. A few days ago she'd wanted to believe they were all like her ex. It had made travelling the high road by herself a bit easier. But…even though Cooper was all sorts of shades of grey…she could tell he was more light than darkness.

'Fine. You got me. I'm trying to tar you all with the same brush.'

'It's a dangerous way to go through life.'

Though the smile remained in place, his voice was weighted with warning. He clearly felt he'd been tarred with too broad a brush at some juncture.

'Do you mean presuming everyone's the same?'

'Exactly.'

The light in his eyes could've been from the fire, but Audrey was pretty certain they were lit from within.

A woman wearing a Puffin Inn apron bustled up to their table. 'Can I get you two anything to drink? A lovely bottle of seasonal red to share between you—? Oh! Cooper. Hi, there. Sorry. I didn't…um… I'm ever so sorry about your gran. I was at the funeral, but I had to get back here after, and as there wasn't a wake—'

'No bother,' Cooper cut in, giving her a curt

nod before looking at Audrey. 'Wine? Soft drink?'

'Hot chocolate,' she said.

'What? With your food?' The woman laughed, then gave Cooper a scolding look. 'Have you not got the heating system working in that Jeep yet? Dr Anstruther told me it was on the blink a few weeks back.'

Cooper shook his head, but offered no explanation.

'Bring it down to my Billy's place and he'll get it working for you in no time.'

Cooper glanced at her sharply.

'Cooper,' the woman said gently, 'he's not the same lad you knew back then. He's a father now. A husband. He's changed a lot.'

Cooper made an indecipherable noise, then said brightly, 'I'll have a Coke, if that's all right. Audrey? Do you know what you'd like to eat?'

'I can recommend the chicken and mushroom pie,' the woman said to Audrey. 'It's actually Cooper's gran's recipe. Absolutely brilliant. Isn't it, Coop? Gertie's chicken and mushroom pie. You must be half made of it, you ate it so much as a lad.'

Cooper kept his eyes fixed to the menu chalkboard and said nothing.

Audrey gave the woman a smile, then said, 'I'll have the pie. It sounds great.'

Cooper briskly asked for steak and chips, looked at Audrey, and then, clearly dissatisfied with his behaviour, reached out and touched the woman's arm before she left. 'Thanks, Fiona. I'll give Billy a ring tomorrow, okay?'

Fiona gave him a smile and a nod, then said their meals would be just a few minutes.

After she'd gone a silence fell over the table, until their drinks were brought over by a young man. 'Here ya are, Coop. Nice to see you back in the Puffin. Mum says to tell you the offer still stands.'

Cooper lifted his chin in acknowledgement, then raised his pint glass to the woman behind the bar. 'I'll let her know, son. Ta.'

'So?' Audrey said after she'd taken a sip of her hot chocolate. 'Are you going to tell me?'

'Tell you what?'

'About all these mysterious conversations.'

He opened his mouth, clearly about to shut her down, then took a swig of his drink and looked her in the eye. 'I've got what you might call a chequered past here on Bourtree.'

'In what way?'

'Just about every way you could imagine.'

'What? Were you the town ruffian?'

'Nope.' He shook his head and took another drink. 'Billy was.'

'What? Nice Billy who's married to our waitress?'

'He used to beat the proverbial hell out of me back in the day,' Cooper said.

You could see the admission was a big one. No man liked to admit they'd been at the wrong end of a fist.

'I'm so sorry, Coop.'

'Don't be.'

'But I don't understand why—'

He cut her off. 'My parents were the island drunks. When you were their kid no one let you forget about the footsteps you were going to follow in.'

'You don't have a drink problem.'

'No. It's the one thing I have to thank them for. I've known first-hand for a long time what alcohol dependency does to a person.' Cooper took another gulp of his soft drink, ran his fingers through his thick hair, then looked her straight in the eye. 'You want the whole story?'

'Only if you want to tell it.'

Her answer clearly caught him by surprise, and that surprise softened him. Took away a layer of the defensiveness he was cloaked in. Enough so that he began to talk.

'My parents should never have been parents...' he began.

He went on to tell her about their romance

at school. Swift, fiery, culminating in a pregnancy—his sister Shona.

'They thought it sounded "fun" to have a baby or two, and then figured out it was more responsibility than fun, so they basically dumped us on my gran. She was my dad's mother, and she said she'd be damned if she'd see the bairns of her son be neglected.'

'What about your mum's parents?'

'They kicked her out when they found out she was pregnant. They'd never had much time for her anyway.'

'In what way?'

He lifted an imaginary bottle of wine and glugged it down.

'Oh.'

'Exactly. They moved to Glasgow years back. Before I was born. More pubs to choose from.'

'So, did you grow up living with your gran or your parents?'

'Both. Sort of. My parents never had enough money to have a place of their own so we all lived at my gran's. When they were around.'

'What do you mean?'

'There wasn't much work for them on the island—not with their reputations. They came back every now and again, when they got their hands on some cash.'

'So…where are they now?'

'Dead.'

The hot chocolate churned uncomfortably round Audrey's stomach. 'I'm sorry.'

'Don't be.' He sounded as if he meant it. 'They'd come back for my thirteenth birthday and left as soon as the candles went out on the cake Gran had made me. They got hammered, went for a drive around the island, forgot to turn on the bend where the island ends and—splash—they ended up in the sea.'

'Oh, Cooper.' Audrey covered her mouth with her hands.

'Honestly, Audrey…' Cooper waved his hand between them, as if he'd just told her he'd ripped his favourite shirt but had bought a new one, so it was fine. 'I've moved on. It's not the problem.'

Audrey stayed silent.

'I owe everything I am today to my grandmother.' His mouth quirked into a crooked smile. 'The good parts, anyway.'

'You must miss her.'

His expression darkened. 'I don't deserve to.'

'Why not? You obviously loved her very much.'

'I didn't show it.'

She and her father had never been hugely demonstrative. It had been more…built in. A given.

'Sometimes love is something you just know. It doesn't need big showy gestures.'

Big showy gestures like the ones Rafael had been prone to. Funny how she only now realised the huge bouquets of flowers and flashy outfits he had had delivered to her at work had always made her squirm rather than make her feel genuinely cherished.

'Audrey…' Cooper reached across and took both of her hands in his, as if he was imploring her to truly hear what he was saying. 'I wasn't here when Gran died. She told me she was sick. I told her she'd be fine, that she was tough as old boots, and then took another double shift. Then another. I told her I'd come on the weekend. Then I didn't. That's what I've done for the past fifteen years—constantly telling her I'd be there for her and not making good on my word. This time I well and truly failed her and there is nothing I can do to make up for it.'

Oh.

'I should've been on the next ferry out of Glasgow.'

'You weren't to know.'

'I knew her cold had turned into a cough. I knew she was eighty. I knew it was winter. I knew I had a hospital full of elderly folk suffering from "wee colds" that had turned into pneumonia—which, in some cases, would kill them.'

* * *

Cooper pulled his hands away from Audrey's. The warm comfort of them was more than he deserved. 'Nothing you say can absolve me. I left the one woman who properly cared for me to die alone.'

'Is that what happened?'

Shards of unbearable pain lanced through his chest. 'Yes.' It was the first time he'd admitted it out loud. 'Dr Anstruther had been checking in on her once a day. As had a couple of neighbours.'

'Had she rung them?'

'No, I had.'

'So you were looking after her the best you could. It sounds as though you were needed at the hospital.'

'Audrey. You're not getting it.' His voice thickened with emotion, but he ploughed on, punctuating each of his sentences with a sound rap on the table with his fist. 'I was needed here. My gran died by herself. There was no one holding her hand. No one making her breathing any easier. No one to tell her how much they appreciated the sacrifices she'd made. Telling her how very much she was lo—'

He cut himself off as a lorry's worth of emotion bashed him in the chest. Crying over his biggest mistake in life wasn't going to bring his grandmother back. Nothing would.

'She may have had a gruff demeanour, but she was the heart of this island. There are signs of her everywhere.'

As if on cue, a beautiful piece of chicken and mushroom pie arrived and was slid in front of Audrey. It was a generous portion, covered in golden pastry. Tiny mushroom-shaped pastry pieces floated in a glossy gravy that pooled around a fluffy mountain of mashed potato. Exactly the way she'd served it to him countless times as a boy. It had been his absolute favourite dish.

In contrast, Cooper's plate was simply what it said on the tin. A steak and some chips. His should've looked the better dish. A more expensive cut of meat. Golden, crunchy, perfectly made chips. A small piece of parsley on top. But somehow the meal he'd chosen didn't come close to matching the lashings of generosity and love he automatically endowed the chicken pie with.

'Want some?' Audrey asked, loading a mouthful of the gravy-rich pie onto her fork.

'No, don't worry.'

'Go on,' she urged, moving the fork towards his lips. 'I think you've earned it.'

He didn't know why, but deep in his heart

he knew Audrey wasn't telling him he'd done a good day's work. She was saying that, despite his flaws, she admired him. That somehow, despite everything, his grandmother had understood he'd been running away from his demons, not from her.

Eyes connected to Audrey's, he accepted the pie. As he did so something pure and intense passed between them. Something vital that gave him the first kernel of belief that one day he might be able to forgive himself. Make some proper changes in his life. Starting with a show of gratitude for the woman who'd raised him.

As if reading his mind, Audrey asked, 'Did you plan on having a wake some day?'

'That's what Fiona was on about. The wake. They offered to let me have it here.'

'A wake is for the other people who loved her. It sounds as though there'd be quite a showing.'

'I don't know... I just wouldn't want it to turn morose. She would've hated people weeping and bemoaning her loss.' She would've set them all to work if that sort of carry-on began. The thought made him smile. Almost.

Audrey gave a half-shrug. 'My parents have both passed away and I found that their wakes were an amazing way to remember all the good things.'

He flinched. His parents' wake had been a disaster. Barely anyone had shown up. It had been him and his gran and a pile of sandwiches no one ate, plus a few neighbours who had popped in more for his gran than for him.

The fact they could've killed someone else as easily as they'd killed themselves had riled the islanders. If ever there was a group of people who looked after one another it was the people of Bourtree. Okay, but it wasn't as if everyone here was sainted. People were people. Some were kind, some less so, and—

He looked across the pub and saw Fiona greeting her husband Billy as he doled out waves and handshakes to the lads at the bar. He said something and they all laughed. Years back the same boys would've hunched over their pints and hoped he wouldn't notice them.

Cooper added 'ability to change' to the list of attributes a human could possess. Even him. But it had to come from inside. Not from a Santa suit.

'Want some more?' Audrey looked down at her plate, then coloured, realising she'd eaten the whole thing. 'Sorry.' She winced, her shoulders creeping up to her ears as she did so.

Cooper smiled, resisting the urge to run a finger along her jawline. There was something about her that got to him. In a good way. Sure, she'd come off the ferry all bristly and elf-resistant…but he could see how meeting a stubble-faced doctor in a Santa suit who dipped in and out of a good mood would've appeared pretty strange. Especially considering she was suffering her own piece of heartache.

He was tempted to ask her about it, but thought it would feel too much like trying to even out the 'bad luck story' playing field.

His phone buzzed in his pocket. 'Sorry.' He held up the phone. 'Work.'

Finlay Anstruther was on the line. The elderly doctor was busy attending an infant with a troubling cough, and he ran him through the facts of a potential emergency and asked if Cooper could attend it.

'Absolutely. We'll be there in two minutes.' He hung up the phone. 'Sorry, we've got to go. Suspected heart attack.'

Audrey was up and out of her seat straight away. They pulled on their jackets, and when Fiona rushed up to see if everything was okay she told them not to worry about the bill—they would sort it out later.

When they got outside, Cooper ran to the Jeep, grabbed the run-bag and the portable AED, shouldered them, then asked, 'Are you up for a wee run? Watch yourself—it's icy.'

Without waiting for a response, he held out his hand to Audrey and began to jog.

A couple of minutes later they arrived at a grey stone building down at the far end of the High Street. It had a bright green door and a colourful Christmas wreath hung around the polished brass knocker. Before they could knock, the door was opened by a distraught woman in her fifties.

'Oh, thank God, Cooper. James is in the lounge.'

Cooper entered, introducing Audrey as he did so. 'Is he still conscious?'

'Aye,' she said, leading them down the corridor. 'He's barely able to move, though. He's clutching his chest, complaining of a terrible pain.'

'Have you rung the emergency services, Karen?'

'Aye, but they say the helicopter's out at one of the other islands and taking him across on the ferry would be—'

Cooper silently finished the sentence. It would be too late.

They entered a large, comfortable-looking lounge at the centre of which was a huge Christmas tree that must've been almost three metres high. Lying on the floor next to it was a very pale middle-aged man with an impressive pot belly.

Cooper dropped to his knees and unshouldered the run-bag, aware that Audrey knelt on the opposite side of him, preparing the AED. The fact James was conscious was a sign this might be a false alarm.

'All right, there, James?'

'Been better, Coop. Sorry about your gran.'

'Aye, well…it's you we're worried about tonight.'

'Cooper?' Audrey had opened the run-bag and found some GTN spray as well as aspirin.

'Thanks, Audrey.' He took the medication, asked James's wife for a glass of water, then returned his focus to James. 'Can you tell me how you're feeling right now?'

'The pain's not so strong now. It was, though. Thought I was on my way to the pearly gates.'

'Hopefully that's some time away yet,' Cooper said, aware that you could never make promises of longevity. He'd called too many times of death in the A&E to think otherwise. 'Shall we get some of these cushions under you to make you a bit more comfortable. Audrey…?'

Without being instructed she deftly put a sofa cushion underneath James's knees and a smaller one under his head.

'Are you taking anything for angina or your heart?'

'No, Coop.' His eyes flicked to the doorway, where his wife was just returning with the water. 'It felt like I was being kicked in the chest with a steel-toed boot. I was up there trying to put the star on the tree. I could barely breathe. Even my jaw felt pain. If Karen hadn't noticed me going white, we could've added concussion to the list.'

'So, you've been decorating your tree, have you?'

'Aye. Up and down the ladder I don't know how many times. Karen likes it just so, and you know the saying…'

Cooper shook his head, heartened that James was able to speak without pausing to get his breath.

'Happy wife…happy life.'

'That's a good saying, James. So…' He took a look at the huge tree. 'How often would you say you do this level of exercise? Going up and down a ladder like that.'

James huffed out a weak laugh. 'Once a year.'

'Have you experienced anything like this before?'

'Aye,' James conceded, and his wife let out a small gasp. 'Only every now and again, love. Usually when we're at a ceilidh or some such. Not the best time to cause a fuss, and it always passes.'

'Fair enough, but bear in mind that not saying anything could have some serious consequences.'

Still in the doorway, Karen asked, 'Is he having a heart attack? Don't you need to use the defibrillator or something?'

Cooper shook his head. 'I don't think so, Karen. We only use the AED for two reasons. One is for folk suffering from ventricular fibrillation. If your James was enduring that, he'd not be conscious. The other is ventricular tachycardia. Basically, his heart would be beating too fast to get blood to all the right places.'

'I think he's saying I wouldn't be jabbering on like I am, love,' James said weakly.

Karen nodded. 'So...?'

Cooper looked at his watch. 'It's been about twenty minutes since you first experienced the chest pain, yes?'

James nodded.

'My educated guess is that you're having a pretty intense angina attack, brought about by physical exertion.'

Karen gasped. 'You mean this is *my* fault?'

'No one's saying that, but short, sharp bursts of exercise when you're not accustomed to it can highlight underlying heart trouble.'

'Like a disease?'

Cooper saw Audrey start to speak, then stop herself. He sat back on his heels and nodded for her to go ahead. She was one half of his team. There was no reason why she shouldn't explain it.

The smile he received in return hit him straight in the chest. She showed a level of gratitude for being 'given the floor' that didn't seem right. As if she was used to having her opinion doubted. Crazy, considering she was clearly very good at her job. More so when you took into account the fact she'd worked in one of London's premier paediatric hospitals.

He was lucky to have her. Doubly so, considering he'd all but poured out his entire life history to her. Something he hadn't done with a single one of his girlfriends back in Glasgow.

The word 'girlfriend' got stuck on a loop in his head. He wondered what sort of girlfriend Audrey was. And, more to the point, what sort of boyfriend would've let her go. A fool, no doubt. Just as he'd be foolish even to think of going there. She was leaving. And he was— Well, he didn't know what he was doing, and the last person on earth a heartbroken nurse needed was him.

'Angina isn't a disease,' Audrey explained to the married couple. 'It can definitely feel like a heart attack, but the pain is actually a reaction to a lack of oxygen-rich blood to the heart.'

'Which he had because he was climbing up the ladder?' asked Karen.

Audrey nodded. 'If you're not used to it, yes. That sort of exertion can provoke an angina attack.'

'How do we stop it? Should he be on bed rest?'

Audrey shook her head and gave Cooper a quick glance. He nodded that she should carry on.

'It's best to get a proper diagnosis. We'll take full notes of what happened tonight and perhaps you should…um… Cooper? What's the protocol here?'

'You'll need to make an appointment at one of the hospitals in Glasgow.'

'Can't you do it?' Karen begged.

'We can do some of the tests. It's what they call a lifestyle assessment. Blood pressure, cholesterol levels, your BMI, your waist size…'

'Ach, Cooper, don't… I know I've eaten one or two extra pieces of pie over the years, but I've done all right.'

Karen sent them imploring looks. 'This is his favourite time of the year. Could he start a diet after Hogmanay, like everyone else?'

'Sounds like Cooper's saying I might be heading into the New Year in a coffin if I did that, love.'

'Whoa!' Cooper waved his hands between them. 'There's no need to head in that direction just yet. How about we go the hospital route? Get a series of checks? Maybe do a little Christmas shopping over in Glasgow?'

'What can they do that Dr Anstruther can't?' Karen asked suspiciously.

Cooper tried to hide a bit of frustration. Why were islanders so dubious about mainland hospitals? They did amazing work there. Saved thousands of lives. More.

Audrey jumped into the silence. 'An electrocardiogram. A coronary angiography…' She ticked off a couple more tests that would help them understand what had happened today. 'Those tests could help save your life.'

Karen burst into tears. 'Oh, James. Forgive me. I'll never ask you to decorate the tree again.'

Audrey hid a smile and Cooper tried his best to do the same. 'It's looking pretty good now,' he said.

They wrote down a few notes, then suggested a daily aspirin to create easier blood flow through the heart's arteries in case they were narrowed.

'Ring straight away if you experience any pain again,' Cooper told James.

After a few more assurances they left the house.

'Good work in there,' Cooper said.

'Just doing my job,' Audrey said, but he could see the compliment had hit its mark. She began to hum a little tune.

'Hey. Is that a Christmas carol you're humming?'

She stopped instantly. 'Oh, my gosh. It is.'

'That's not a bad thing, you know. As they say, 'tis the season.'

She pulled a face. 'For most people. Not so much for me.'

Cooper took a risk. 'Does this have anything to do with the heartbreak you told Cayley you were busy healing?'

Audrey winced. 'She told you that?'

'Sorry. Doctor-patient confidentiality doesn't seem to work the other way around. At least not when you need it to. Want to talk about it?'

Audrey waited until Cooper had opened up the back of the Jeep and swung the run-bag in to answer. 'Maybe...'

He gave her a nod. 'Zip up that warm coat of yours. I know the perfect place for a confidential talk. Jump in.'

CHAPTER SIX

'WHERE ARE YOU taking me?' Audrey wasn't nervous exactly, but… Okay, maybe a little.

'Here,' Cooper said, pulling off the coastal route to a viewing point at the north end of the island. He parked the vehicle so that it faced the sea.

'Dark out tonight,' Audrey said, looking for the moon and finding only the tiniest of slivers.

'Perfect.'

'For what?' She poked Cooper in the arm. 'What's with the aura of mystery?'

'You'll see.' Cooper smiled, undid his seatbelt and leant on the steering wheel to peer up at the sky. 'No light pollution up here. I imagine it's all Christmas lights and dazzle down in London.'

Audrey's nerve-endings crackled. 'Pretty much.'

'Ex-boyfriend in London, too?' Cooper asked.

His eyes were still on the sky which, now that she looked, Audrey could see was alight with stars. The incredible beauty of it took the edge off admitting, 'Ex-fiancé.'

'Ah.'

'I found him rocking an elf by the Christmas tree after a Christmas party hop.'

He gave her a rueful smile. 'That explains why you weren't keen to wear the elf costume.'

'Yup!'

She dug into her coat pockets and pulled out her gloves. As she worked each finger into place, she told him the rest. They'd been due to be married on Christmas Eve. She'd been stupid enough to insist upon paying for the wedding. Now she was jobless, and homeless—apart from this locum post and a room in his gran's house for the duration!

'You lived together?' he asked.

She nodded. 'I'd just sold my parents' house. Well…my house after my dad passed. Someone else's house now. I'd moved in with Rafael two weeks earlier.'

For the first time she felt a proper burst of anger.

'He didn't even let me unpack my personal knick-knacks. Said the flat was fine as it was. What kind of person does that? And what kind of idiot doesn't take it as a massive warning sign that things aren't going well? Maybe I knew all along. Maybe I wasn't unpacking things because there was a part of me that knew none of it was meant to be. Or maybe I'm reading too much into it. You haven't exactly changed your grandmother's place around…'

Cooper gave her a soft smile. 'I'm not changing my grandmother's place because I want to preserve what I can't have any more.'

Audrey's breath caught and constricted in her throat. 'Do you think that's what Rafael was doing? Preserving what he thought he couldn't have any more?'

Cooper shrugged. 'I wouldn't presume to guess, but the fact he cheated so quickly does suggest his heart wasn't in it.'

'But he's the one who proposed! We'd only been dating for three months!' Audrey yanked her voice down from screeching fury to simmering rage. 'He's the one who wined and dined me. The one who convinced me to leave my job and work in paediatrics. I couldn't really believe any of it was happening, to be perfectly honest. It felt…surreal.'

When what it should have felt like was a dream come true.

'So…' Cooper turned to face her, his expression not filled with pity, as she'd feared, more with empathy. 'Does that mean somewhere in your heart you knew it wasn't right?'

'No!' Audrey spat, and then, as if she was a

newly filled balloon someone had forgotten to tie off, she deflated against the car seat. 'Yes. Maybe… I don't know. He was so different from the men I normally dated. Not that there were dozens of them or anything.'

'Different in what way?'

'Dashing. Rich. Famous.'

'A surgeon?'

'Yes.' She said his surname.

Cooper let out a low whistle.

'See? I told you.'

'Well…' Cooper looked back out to the stars. 'I don't know if this is going to make you feel any better, but the words you use to describe him aren't the words I would use.'

'Why? What would you use?'

'Arrogant. Opportunist. Lothario.' He took a breath and held it for a moment, as if debating whether or not to say the final part. 'In search of a British passport.'

Audrey's blood ran cold. 'What?'

'Look…' Cooper put up his hands. 'I don't know the guy from Adam, but I do know his reputation. We get patients who demand the best, and from what I hear your man there is an incredible heart surgeon. But he also *breaks* hearts.'

'Well, yeah. Obviously,' Audrey huffed.

'I'm talking about back in Argentina.'

'How do you know anything about Argentinian heart surgeons?'

He looked out to the sky again, grabbed a
cloth from the car door pocket and rubbed the
windscreen clear. 'Six degrees of separation, I
guess.'

'What?' Now Audrey was getting properly
confused.

'I went to a conference on emergency medicine a few months back.'

'So?'

'In Argentina.'

'Ah.'

'Your man—'

'He's not my man,' she snapped.

'Right you are. Apologies. Mr de Leon was
there and, as such, so was the rumour mill. I
didn't pay any attention to it at the time because, as you know, I know how harmful gossip can be.'

'What was it?'

'You're sure you want to know?'

'If it will help me understand why he did what
he did, then go for it. Tell me everything.'

Cooper nodded. 'Over there he worked at the
country's most exclusive hospital. His patients
were politicians, film stars, Argentina's equivalent of royalty.'

'He's not up for malpractice, is he?'

'No,' Cooper said, and then quickly explained. 'He didn't only have access to his patients, according to those who worked with him. It seems he also had regular access to wives while their husbands were recovering in hospital. One of those wives turned out to be married to someone pretty high up in the government. A man who could make a medical licence disappear if he wanted to.'

Each of Cooper's words was like a little dagger in her heart. She had been conned.

She barely recognised her own voice as she asked, 'So he came to the UK to get citizenship in case his world crashed over there?'

'Looks like it. He definitely didn't lose his licence, because the UK is strict on that. But his reputation with women isn't nearly as golden as his surgical reputation. I know it's painful, but I hope it makes what he did seem less personal.'

It made her feel like a proper idiot—that was what it did. 'You must think I am the most naïve person to walk the earth.'

'Not at all,' Cooper said, with an intensity that made her look up and meet his eyes. 'You were conned by an expert.'

'It just feels so…' she sought the right word and could only come up with '…icky.'

'I know.'

'How?' Audrey barked a mirthless laugh. 'How on earth can you know?'

He pulled off his woollen hat and gave his head a scrub before tugging it back on. 'I suppose because I've been a bit of a conman myself.'

'How do you mean?'

'I told my grandmother that I'd be back to see her countless times. That I loved her.'

'Cooper. You obviously loved her. Anyone can see that.'

'But I didn't make good on my word. Having her die the way she did, alone, made me take a really hard look in the mirror.'

'And what you saw was Santa?'

They both stared at one another and then, unexpectedly, began to laugh. Proper belly laughs that carried on for ages—until all of a sudden Cooper looked out of the window and said, 'Quick! Get out.'

He leapt out of the car with such urgency Audrey followed suit.

'Here.' Cooper beckoned to her. 'Come and have a look.'

He held his arm out and, when she approached, put it around her shoulders then tugged her close to him, as if he'd been doing it for years. He pointed up to the skies and there, dancing in the heavens, were the most beautiful, celestial lights she'd ever seen. Greens, reds, golds. The colours of Christmas.

'It's the aurora borealis,' he explained, his arm still round her shoulders as if it belonged there.

It felt so nice she had to resist the urge to snuggle into him. Wrap her arms round his waist. Which was just plain wrong, considering she'd vowed not even to *think* about a man, let alone cuddle up to one until she got herself back to being the Audrey she respected.

A moment's weakness, she told herself. She'd just poured her heart out to him. And the fact he didn't think she was pathetic for falling for such a duplicitous conman had touched her. That and the fact she was drawn to him. To a man who understood what it felt like to love and lose and then wonder how on earth to get up again.

'The Vikings thought the northern lights were a reflection of the Valkyries' armour as they went into battle,' Cooper said, his blue eyes still trained on the heavens.

'Sounds scary.'

Cooper gave a little shrug. 'Apparently dying in battle was a great honour.'

Audrey snorted. 'I'd prefer to delay that honour for quite some time, thank you very much.'

'Now, that sounds like a woman who is taking charge of her own life,' he said.

A bloom of hope swirled round her heart. 'You think?'

'Absolutely.' Cooper looked down at her, his expression shifting. 'Do you want my honest opinion?'

Not it if involved kissing. His lips were so close…

She was staring at them as she said, 'I think I'm going to get it, whether or not I want it.'

He gave a good-natured laugh. 'Fair enough. I was thinking that for someone who's endured a broken engagement so recently…you seem more angry than heartbroken. Are you sure you were properly in love with the guy? Perhaps it was more—and don't take this the wrong way, because I'm not judging you—that you might've been in love with the *idea* of him?'

It was a good point.

She'd been so swept off her feet she'd barely had time to think these past few months. She'd had boyfriends before, but they'd never showered her with so many gifts and sweet nothings. With beautiful bouquets of flowers that had blinded her to the truth. Flowers wilted. Sweet nothings were exactly that. And that fancy flat he'd asked her to move into hadn't been a home.

Not like Cooper's gran's house was, anyway. Gertie's home gave an instant sense of comfort and healing.

Why had she fallen for such artifice? It wasn't like her. Not at all.

Had it been the promise of a family? An identity? Or the promise of being loved as much as her father had clearly loved her mother. The mother she'd never really known.

She thought back to those final days with her father. His insistence that Audrey must never settle for second best when it came to love. Never, ever compromise who she was, because true love didn't mean losing yourself. It meant becoming a better version of yourself than you'd ever believed possible.

She'd sure messed that up.

She looked up to the skies and thought of those ancient warriors heading off to battle. It was an interesting way to see the mesmeric whorls and flashes of colour. Proud and strong instead of fleeting and inaccessible.

Perhaps instead of writing her story as that of a wronged woman fleeing a humiliating situation, she owed herself a different version. Sure, she'd left with tears streaking her cheeks and remarkably little to her name, but she still had her name. Her nursing skills. Enough pride to get herself a job, a place to stay and to make a vow never to let herself be hurt that way again.

She'd already helped some of the people here on Bourtree Castle through the type of nursing she loved. And, although living with Cooper hadn't been part of the plan, in a way it was good to have someone else there. Surprise hot chocolate in bed was far better than sobbing herself to sleep at night.

Two wounded warriors seeking a new life…

A gust of arctic wind blew in from the sea. Audrey shivered. Cooper pulled her in a bit closer to him. She turned towards him, and as if by unspoken agreement he turned to her.

As their eyes met a heated pulse of electricity flashed between them and grew taut.

Cooper was very good-looking. More so than she'd initially given him credit for, given the whole Santa suit thing and…

Oh…wait a minute. Was he…?

Cooper was tipping his head towards hers. Audrey's heart began to pound. Was he going to kiss her?

The sound of blood rushing through her nervous system drowned out the sound of the waves as he reached out and tucked a stray tendril of her pixie cut behind her ear. Her skin felt as though it had been brushed by the same light that coloured the skies. Their bodies shifted slightly. They were aligning themselves so that…yes…their heads could ease into place for what surely had to be a kiss.

Did she want this? Her body seemed to. Did her heart?

Her brain made a loud, plaintive cry that travelled straight to her gut. What did her heart know? It had fallen for a complete idiot. A liar. A Christmas romance was not the wisest way to embark on her new life…whatever that might be. If this kiss happened, it would definitely be a rebound kiss.

She looked deep into Cooper's eyes for a sign. Something—anything—to say that whatever was happening between them was genuine. She didn't see promises, but she saw kindness and respect. Two things she now knew for certain hadn't existed in her last relationship.

He shifted so that one of his hands spread across the centre of her back and the second slid along her waist. They were standing closer than they ever had before. So close she could feel his warm breath upon her mouth. Feel the pounding of his heartrate as it matched her accelerated pulse. Her lips parted, her body all but making the decision for her.

At the last minute, just as her lips began to physically ache for his touch, for the completion of a kiss, he dropped his arms from around her and took hold of her hand. Together, silently, they leant back against the big Jeep, her heart still pounding.

It was the right decision. One Cooper had been strong enough to make for both of them. It was a strength she'd have to develop if she didn't want her life to come crashing down around her again. She wasn't staying here. Cooper might be. He might not be. He didn't know.

They watched the lights weave and wend their way through the heavens with a new powerful energy coursing between the pair of them. As if the mesmeric lights had stamped an indelible mark on her and Cooper, uniting them for ever in this one magic moment. A moment of power. A moment of possibility.

'Right!' Cooper clapped his hands together and gave them a rub as they finished washing and putting away their supper dishes. 'How do you feel about gingerbread men?'

Audrey flopped down onto a cushioned kitchen chair with a grin. 'If you're offering to give me a plate of them with a huge mug of tea I'm all for 'em. I'm pooped.'

'Not surprised. It's been a busy couple of weeks.'

Audrey swept her fingers through her pixie cut, leaving a couple of locks of dark hair sticking out in adorably errant revolt. 'Is it always this busy on the island?'

Cooper gave a little shrug. 'To be honest, I'm

not really sure. I know the islands struggle in general, but Dr Anstruther's been here for ever. As has Noreen, to be fair. The two of them are public health battle axes. Undeterrable. Who knows? Maybe now that we're around, more folk are calling in.'

Audrey made a hard to decipher noise. 'Difficult shoes to fill. Dr Anstruther's, anyway. I take it Noreen is coming back?'

'Oh, aye. Unless this whole grandmother thing pulls her to Australia permanently she'll be here for years yet. She's one of those women who claims she'll retire when she's dead.'

'It'll be a lot of work for her, with Doc A retiring.'

It would be a lot of work for a new doctor, too. But that wasn't the problem. The job of an island doctor wasn't just a full-time GP role. It was more… It was a calling. Community service. Above and beyond the regular oath of a doctor to do no harm. It was *being there* when people needed you most.

Not his forte.

But could it be? It wasn't as if anyone had pushed him behind the bike shed since his return. Taken a pop at him for having parents who didn't make the grade. Quite the opposite. He'd been welcomed with open arms. Arms he'd

spent a lifetime telling himself he didn't deserve
to be embraced by.

He slammed the door shut on those thoughts
and did what he did best: focused on the here
and now.

He gave Audrey a grin. 'All of which is precisely why we need a good biscuit fix.'

Audrey laughed and toed off her ankle boots.
'And where exactly is this magic plate of restor-
ative biscuits going to appear from? Down the
chimney?'

Cooper gave his eyebrows an impish jig. 'Me.
And you. If you want to give me a hand?'

Audrey gave him a sidelong look.

A couple of weeks ago he would've caught a
healthy dose of scepticism in those chocolatey
brown eyes of hers. Today the look was more
impish. Playful. Not as heated as that moment
they'd shared beneath the aurora borealis, but
he caught glimmers of that now and again—
just as he was sure she saw glimmers of what
was clearly a shared attraction in his own eyes.

Yes, things between the two of them had
been…*interesting* since that night. And by 'interesting' he meant two weeks of loaded looks
and his bloodstream lighting up like a Christmas tree every time their hands brushed—with
or without gloves—and lots of weird throat-
clearing when their eyes locked over some

shared commonality only for them to remember they were in front of patients who needed their assistance.

'What are you actually talking about, Coop?'

He smiled.

That was another thing. Somehow over the past fortnight he'd become Coop, rather than Cooper. Dr Anstruther had become Dr A. And their regular patients, if they were happy with it, were also referred to by nicknames.

In short, Audrey had been accepted by the islanders with open arms. No more suspicious, 'Where's Noreen?' when she came in. It was smiles and hugs and promises to pass on information about how to make Helen's Scottish Tablet or Mr Gibbon's black pudding bonbons. The fact they'd even had to make supper tonight had been a change. Most of their patients were so busy plying them with seasonal nibbles they came home stuffed and ready for bed.

Another awkward time. They were always loitering at the bottom of the stairs, reminding each other of 'just one last thing' before yawns and fatigue finally forced them to their own rooms.

Cooper reached into a cabinet and pulled out a homemade scrap book. Inside were the recipes that had literally made him the man he was today. He placed it on the table in front of Audrey.

He could tell Audrey was aware that the book was precious to him. She wiped her hands on a tea towel, gave him a wide-eyed look and then, hands aloft over the thick coloured cardboard cover, asked, 'May I?'

'Please.' He nodded at the book, which had his grandmother's script all over it except for the cover, where she'd used stencils: *Gertie's Good Eats*, it read. And they certainly were.

He pulled out the chair next to Audrey and sat down.

'Are these all of your grandmother's recipes?'

'That they are.'

Audrey made a low *ooh* noise, then asked, 'The chicken pie is in here?'

Cooper nodded.

'Want to make it one night?'

He sucked in a sharp breath and Audrey instantly fell over herself apologising. 'Sorry. I shouldn't push. I know we've talked about her a bit…but it still must be hard. Living here. Seeing signs of her every day but not actually seeing *her*.'

Cooper nodded. 'It is. Sometimes I can't bear it. But I hate that I wasn't with her at the end even more.'

Audrey gave his hand a squeeze but said

nothing. What could she say? He'd messed up one of those things you should get right. The only thing he could change now was himself.

He looked at Audrey as she began to flip through the pages. *She would be worth changing for.* He checked the thought. Change came from within and had to be composed of purity of intent. Otherwise... Well, you'd end up where Audrey was. Seeking solace from a romance that had been a mirage.

Was that what this was to him? A romance? *No...* Was it?

He definitely enjoyed their verbal sparring. And the way they'd worked together as a team pretty much from the start. She had the guts to stand up to him. The courage to press her patients for the truth. She was firm but fair. Like his gran. She was incredibly beautiful. And also very vulnerable. She deserved someone with a solid foundation. Someone who came from a good family with kind, warm hearts. Not a man who problem-solved by moving away from things that troubled him instead of facing them head-on. Owning his mistakes like a man.

Or was that what this was? Working here on Bourtree? Owning his mistakes... Was this him working towards being the type of man a woman like Audrey could love?

Ach. Too intense. They were meant to be making biscuits.

He clapped his hands together. 'I thought we'd pick up one of Gran's traditions so that the islanders know that we—that I—well, that some of Gertie's traditions are still alive and well.'

'And you're talking about gingerbread men?'

'Aye. And snowballs and chocolate crinkle biscuits and jammy stars and—'

Audrey started laughing and waving her hands. 'Wait a minute. I don't know about you, but I'm not much of a baker. Wouldn't we be better off going down to the bakery and buying them?'

'Absolutely not. Homemade is the only way when you're a MacAskill.'

'Er… Cooper? I hate to point out the obvious, but… I'm not a MacAskill.'

Her tone was light, but when their eyes met their gazes held with a magnetic tension.

She could be. Of all the women he'd known, Audrey was the strongest contender. But he wasn't ready. Might never be.

For her sake he broke the eye contact. She deserved better.

'Ach,' he said, with a dramatic sweep of his hand. 'You're living here. Consider yourself an honorary MacAskill.'

Something lit up in her eyes that he couldn't

quite identify, but it felt positive. As if being an honorary MacAskill worked for her. For now, anyway.

Cooper pushed his chair back onto its back legs and gave her a faux shocked grin. 'So... Are you up for putting a bit of flour and butter together for the islanders?'

'And sugar and baking soda and who knows what else?' Audrey shot back, her voice bubbling with laughter.

'That's what Gertie's recipe book is for. To guide us along the way.'

She'd promised it to him years back. Said that when she was gone it would keep him well fed. On the straight and narrow.

'So...' Audrey shot him a cheeky grin. 'I suppose you're going to tell me you grew up making these biscuits every year and you're an expert?'

The smile dropped from his lips. No. He hadn't. It was one of an increasing bouquet of regrets jammed into his conscience.

His gran had used these biscuits to lure him out of his room after he'd been teased about his parents being pulled over by the police for being drunk and disorderly. To bribe him to come out in the car with her as she took plate after plate of Christmas treats to 'folk less fortunate' when his father had been fired from yet another job. She'd even made them out of season for the entire week between his parents' dying and the funeral.

A funeral, he had to remind himself, that had been for her son and her daughter-in-law. She must've been in deep mourning herself, and all the time she'd risen above her own sorrow to tend to his.

He'd never forget what she'd said as they lowered his father's casket into the ground. She'd taken Cooper's hand in hers, fixed him with a steely gaze and said, 'I'll get it right with you, son. I've made my mistakes. Now let's see if I can get it right.'

'Hey…' Audrey gave his leg a tap, her voice reflecting his change in mood, and then picked up the book. 'Let's try. What's the worst that could happen?'

His becoming everything his grandmother had feared. Lonely, angry, furious at the world for being dealt a poor hand.

He looked down at the book, at his gran's scrawling penmanship, and saw nothing but love and dedication in each page. In each addendum to a measurement. Each little note scribbled on the margin.

Double vanilla if baking for Coop!

He'd change. He'd dig down to his very essence and become the man his grandmother had believed he could be.

Two hours later, Audrey and Cooper had discovered that they were both pretty terrible in the baking department. Regardless, making the biscuits together had lifted the gloomy atmosphere and elevated it to something bright and optimistic.

Now Audrey was lifting a deformed snowman—or was it a reindeer—?to her mouth as Cooper watched. 'You're brave.'

'We'll see just how brave in a minute.' She took a bite, chewed, and then smiled. 'Well, they look horrible, but they taste amazing.'

Cooper nodded and grinned. 'Maybe we should've chilled the dough overnight, as the recipe recommended.'

They both looked down at the handwritten note alongside the typewritten recipe that said, *Do not ignore!*

Audrey wiped her hands again, then began flipping through the pages. 'Maybe we can find an easier one.'

'One that suits the brain power of an A&E doc and a super-nurse?'

Audrey smiled up at him, the compliment clearly hitting its mark. He liked making her feel good. Bringing a smile to her lips. There was something...something inherently *honest* about who she was.

When he let himself think about how badly she'd been treated it made his blood boil. But, though they didn't talk about it too much, he got the sense that Audrey was well and truly prepared to leave the past where it was and do her best to move on. Perhaps he should take a page out of her book.

'This sounds good,' Audrey said, pointing to a recipe for Scottish Rarebit. 'What makes it Scottish?'

Cooper laughed. 'You know how Gran liked mustard more than just about anything?'

She crinkled her brow, then brightened. 'Oh, yes. You said it was in the chicken and mushroom pie, didn't you?'

'Yup. That's French mustard. The main difference between Welsh rarebit and Gran's is an extra wallop of the strong stuff.'

'Mustard?'

'Her own special homemade mustard.'

He tapped the side of his nose, then went to a cupboard, pulling out one of three jars that still remained. It'd be a tough day when he hit the last one.

Audrey read the label and laughed. 'This sounds like it'd put hairs on your chest.'

He cracked the lid open and took a spoon from the cutlery drawer. 'Care to find out?'

'What?' Audrey giggled. 'See if Gertie's Blow-Your-Socks-Off Whisky Mustard puts hairs on my chest? I don't know if I'm brave enough.'

The flirty atmosphere that had been dancing around them for the past couple of weeks ratcheted up a notch.

'You're brave enough,' Cooper said, meaning it. 'You shouldn't doubt yourself. Ever.'

A glint of pride lightened her dark eyes.

It felt good to know he'd put it there.

Not many women could leap from district nursing to a high-stakes paediatric hospital and then slip straight back into district nursing without so much as a blink of an eye.

If he'd met her at the hospital he would've asked her out. He also would've been guaranteed to mess up the relationship. Adding yet another woman to the list of girlfriends he'd disappointed. Perhaps that was why he'd met her now. When he was straddling the fault lines of the path he'd been walking. He could either let himself fall into the abyss or shore up his reserves and leap to solid ground.

'Do you really think so?' Audrey's gaze softened, but still held his.

The energy crackling between them intensified.

'It put hairs on *my* chest.' His voice dropped a notch and the space between them somehow closed. 'The mustard,' he added, for only one reason. To stop himself from kissing Audrey right this very moment.

'I think that's probably a good reason for me not to try it,' Audrey said, her voice barely a whisper.

Cooper put down the jar and cupped Audrey's beautiful face in his hands. He of all people should know that time was precious. 'I want to kiss you.'

Her breath caught in her throat. Cooper could feel her pulse accelerating beneath his touch.

She nodded.

'Is that all right?'

She nodded again.

When their lips met it was as if the rest of the world slipped away. Gravity, time, place…they all disappeared. And in their place was touch, scent and an all-encompassing warmth.

Their light kiss deepened. Heat, energy, intention. Three elements of a kiss that all but melted them together. She tasted of cinnamon and cloves. Of the crisp island air. She smelt of nutmeg and oranges. For the rest of his life he knew those things would be evocative of Audrey.

As he pulled her closer to him, her hands slipped between them and took purchase on his chest. But she wasn't pushing him away. She was feeling the pounding of his heart as it bashed against his ribcage.

'Where do you see this going?' she asked, her lips moving against his.

'I—' He didn't know. 'My plan was to stay here. Take over from Dr Anstruther.'

'Was...?'

'Is.'

And at this exact moment it felt like the truth. He wanted it to be his truth. Would staying right the wrongs of his past? It would only work if it was well and truly what he wanted to do.

She blinked a few times. 'Have you told him that?'

'Not strictly speaking.'

She pulled back. 'Which means...no, you haven't told him?'

Cooper nodded. 'There hasn't been the right time.'

'He's retiring on Christmas Eve, Cooper. The island won't have a doctor.'

Fifteen years of defensiveness flew up to protect him. He fought against it. 'I know. There's an island a bit further down the coast that lost their doctor three years back and they've yet to replace him.'

'But you're not there. And stringing everyone along isn't exactly helping, is it?'

'I'm not stringing anyone along.'

'Well, why not call Dr Anstruther right now and tell him you want the job?'

And therein lay the problem. He would only make that call when he knew he could give the islanders one hundred per cent follow-through.

He missed the A&E. Missed the buzz of it. But already he knew he'd also miss practising medicine on the island. It was making him a better doctor. Having the time to talk and listen to his patients, properly made a real difference.

But there was a very real possibility the only reason he was loving it was because of Audrey. It was a moment in time—just like one of those snow globes you shook up and watched until the magic came to an end. Audrey had arrived when he'd needed some outside perspective, but she would be leaving. No-nonsense Noreen would be back in the new year. Dr Anstruther would leave. As would Audrey.

And then what? Was a life here without her what he wanted? Was a life *with* her—anywhere—what he wanted?

He brushed her hair back from her forehead and dropped a kiss on it. 'I know I don't want to hurt you. But as for the rest of my life… The honest answer is I don't know.'

'Me neither,' she said sadly. 'A rebound for me? A way to move beyond grief for you? Not exactly an ideal love-match.'

Their eyes met again, their arms tangling loosely round each other's waist… Each of them was no doubt thinking, *Is that what this is? A love-match?*

'Want a hot chocolate?' he asked, instead of probing deeper.

She nodded. 'And then I think we'd probably better pretend this didn't happen.'

'You sure?' It hurt to hear her take the practical tack…but it also made sense.

'No… But it's not going anywhere, Coop. So what's the point?'

'Temporary pleasure?' Even as he spoke, he knew it was the wrong thing to say.

'I'll get my temporary pleasure from the hot chocolate, thank you very much.'

'You're a wise woman.'

As she turned around he barely heard her, but just caught the whispered words…

'I hope so.'

CHAPTER SEVEN

'So, YOU THINK that's something you might be interested in, dearie?'

Dr Anstruther's wife, Emily, glanced over Audrey's shoulder as if the pair of them were having a top-secret conversation and sharing MI6 information. For Bourtree, Audrey supposed it was.

Audrey was thrilled to bits they'd thought of her—but, hearing a certain Scottish brogue in her head talking about islanders not taking to change, she asked, 'You're absolutely sure it won't put anyone's nose out of joint?' And by 'anyone' she meant Cooper.

'Not at all. And the costume would fit you perfectly.'

Audrey looked at it again and had to agree. Not that anyone would know it was her, but... 'It would be my pleasure.'

She meant it, too. She'd only been here a few weeks, and already she felt more a member of this community than she had at her own home in London. Maybe she and her father had been too much of a self-contained unit after her mum's death. Too frightened to branch out and, in her father's case, love again in case they were blindsided by another devastating loss.

She hoped she wasn't doing that by being here. Teaching herself to close herself off to possibility. To love.

She thought of the kisses she and Cooper had shared, that she had stopped by demanding to know where he thought things were heading. How would he know? It was one kiss. How could she know? She wouldn't have a job in less than a fortnight. How could anyone know anything?

She smiled at the older woman next to her, about to sell her home of forty-seven years and move to Cornwall 'just to see what excitement lurks on the other tip of Great Britain'. She should take a page out of her book. Seize the day. Seize days that didn't include Argentinian fiancés with a penchant for fancy wine and slinky elf costumes.

Emily adjusted herself so that she was standing by Audrey's side. The two of them took in the hustle and bustle of the large church hall.

'Amazing to think all this chaos will be transformed into the Nativity in fewer than forty-eight hours.' Emily shook her head in disbelief, but the glint of pride in her eyes suggested she knew it would happen.

Audrey grinned. It was pandemonium. Hammers were clanging nails into place, groups of children were off in opposing corners of the hall singing entirely different songs. A man was trying to guide a donkey away from a table that held a dazzling display of Christmas biscuits… not hers and Cooper's, it had to be said.

'Is it normally this…um…?' Audrey tried to find a word for mayhem that sounded nice.

'Chaotic?' Emily filled in for her with a smile. 'Yes. Every year. Although there usually aren't so many people.'

'No?'

'Well, as Cooper may have told you, his grandmother Gertie was the driving force behind the Nativity. Those biscuits of hers had a lot to answer for.'

Audrey had gleaned as much—more from the patients than from Cooper, who only talked about his grandmother in stilted intervals. She got it. It had taken her ages to tell a story about her dad after he'd passed away without bursting into tears.

'You two make quite the team.' Emily gave Audrey's arm a pat.

Audrey's brow crinkled. Did she know about the kiss? Cautiously, she asked, 'In what way?'

Emily pointed across the hall to where Jimmy Tarbot was lugging a huge lantern towards the big doors that led to the church. 'We've not seen Jimmy out and about for years now, really.'

Audrey was about to say that all Cooper had done was suggest he come to the hall, but maybe it had been the magic combination of lone wolf Cooper making the suggestion, the GP's surgery being relocated to the church hall during Nativity season and…if she wasn't mistaken… the very pretty woman who was setting out a huge bowl of fruit at the end of the coffee and tea table.

'Who's she?'

'Angela. She works down the local bakery.'

'Ah…' Audrey smiled, connecting the dots.

'Anyway, young lassie…' Emily gave her arm a little pat. 'I'd best be off. You'll keep our little talk to yourself, won't you?'

Audrey made a *my lips are sealed* gesture, then threw away the imaginary key. Smiling, she sat back down to look at the costume she'd promised to 'attach some dazzle' to.

Twenty minutes later, she hadn't made much progress.

'Ouch!' Audrey pulled her finger away from

the sparkly fabric. Yup... She'd just stabbed herself hard enough to draw blood.

She popped her finger in her mouth and stared at the hem of the cape she was sewing. And by 'sewing' she meant *trying* to sew. Needlecraft was definitely not her speciality.

This whole thing of her and Coop keeping themselves busy so they could avoid the elephant in Gertie's house was beginning to fray at the edges. First it had been work—but they had proved such an efficient team that only the odd out-of-hours emergency required their presence. Then it had been cleaning out the surgery in advance of the builders getting in there—but the builders had decided it wasn't safe for them and that the whole project would have to wait until the New Year, so that the new GP could decide how he or she would like things.

That had thrown a spotlight on the fact that Cooper had yet to pin his name to the job. Which was annoying, because if he did she would know once and for all that she was leaving and he was staying and their paths would never cross again. Or, if he refused the job, she could possibly sound out Dr Anstruther about staying on to help Noreen until they got a new GP.

She tried to tackle the costume's hem again,

succeeding only in having to pull the stitches out. 'Urgh!'

'Is that costume playing silly buggers with you?'

Cooper appeared from behind a large chunk of plywood cut into the shape of a camel. He saw her notice the shape, and pretended to be riding it. Goofball.

'It's a better effort than our Christmas biscuits, isn't it?'

She wanted to laugh. Of course she did. To laugh and pull him towards her, to kiss him and let the world fade into soft focus so she could tell him how much she cared for him. How she'd realised that her feelings were stronger than she'd thought ever since they'd kissed. Kissing that she'd stopped because suffering two broken hearts in a matter of weeks had seemed ridiculous.

Although this whole *not* kissing thing wasn't really working for her either. She was all for a bit of denial, but something was telling her that despite her very best efforts she was falling for Cooper MacAskill.

'Need a plaster?' Cooper leant in, and the scent of island fir and spiced mince pies swirled in along with him. 'Or shall I get out my suture kit?'

'I think we were assigned the wrong jobs,'

Audrey replied dryly, lifting the needle and cloth between them. 'How did I end up doing this and you on props? I thought doctors were the ones who were good at stitching?'

'I would love to show you my excellent stitching skills...' Cooper grinned, sending an unwanted trill of response round her tummy '...but I'm afraid Cayley has demanded I supply her with three camels immediately.'

'Cayley?' Audrey sat up straighter, letting the gold fabric fall onto her lap. 'I thought she was on costumes, like me.'

'Nope. She did it for a day or two, then spotted an open tin of paint and, according to Dr Anstruther, it was love at first sight.' Cooper nodded towards the far end of the church hall where Cayley was buttoning herself into a paint splattered coverall. 'She's been down here every day, apparently. When she's not doing her homework.'

He dropped Audrey a wink that made some butterflies flutter to life and take flight around her heart. His eyes dropped to her finger.

'So what's the situation? Are we counting you amongst the walking wounded?'

'Sitting wounded, more like.'

He knelt down beside her, leaned the camel up against the wall and took her hand in his.

Her instinct was to yank her hand away and

snap *I'm fine, leave it*. Completely counterintuitive to the butterflies now tripping the light fantastic around her insides.

But Cooper had been nothing less than a gentleman since their kitchen kiss. Why would he suddenly opt for a public show of unwanted affection here, in the centre of the church hall?

Cooper pulled her hand up close to his face, presumably to look at it. The hum and whirr of activity round them blurred into a warm buzz, fuelling the growing intensity of the moment. His fingers traced the length of the one she'd pricked. A whoosh of tingles skittered up her arm and across her collarbones.

'Do you think I'll make it?' she asked, her voice little more than a whisper.

'There's one medicine I'd prescribe.' His eyes met hers and held tight.

'Oh?'

His lips lowered, and they were just about to reach her fingertip, her entire body buzzing with anticipation, when someone called out, 'It's snowing!'

A flash of something that looked like disappointment swept through Cooper's eyes before his smile returned. He pushed himself back up to stand and offered her his hand. 'Care to see a rare event out here on Bourtree?'

'What? It doesn't often snow here?'

'Not regularly. Looks like the Christmas fa-eries are intent on you having a magical Christ-mas whether you want it or not.'

She was about to protest, and then remem-bered how grumpy and anti-Christmas she'd been when she'd landed on Bourtree. Funny how hating Christmas had been replaced by so many other things. Positive things. Like caring for their patients. Learning who liked their tea which way and why. Making biscuits with Coo-per. Seeing the aurora borealis with Cooper.

She forced herself to stop. The whole point of her 'exile' to Bourtree had been to discover who she was. Not start another relationship.

Which made feeling Cooper's warm, support-ive hand round hers that much more difficult.

When her hand had been in her ex's she'd felt helpless. As if she'd lost her own life skills and become reliant upon him to guide her through the maze of his world. A world that hadn't felt as warm as this one. In short, it hadn't been a love that had given her confidence. Far from it.

There was, of course, another way to explain why she and Cooper were drawn to each other. They were both broken. She by being hood-winked and Cooper by having his eye on the wrong prize. But, as Cooper often told his pa-tients, once they were healed they'd be stron-ger than ever.

Was that how it would work with her heart? As each day passed she thought less and less of Rafael and more about the life she wanted to live. A life that was honest and simple. A life filled with love and community. A life pretty close to the one she was living now.

Cooper dipped his head so he could look into her eyes. 'You snow-averse?'

'No, not at all,' she said. 'Let's go out there and see if there's enough for a snowball fight.'

He feigned shock. 'I thought you'd be more of a snow angel girl myself.'

The comment flooded her heart with warmth. 'Maybe a bit of both?'

'Well, let's find out.'

Out on the High Street, with the lights twinkling, the Christmas tree glowing up at the castle ruins, and the scent of mulled wine coming from The Puffin, Cooper couldn't help but feel as though he was part of something special. Particularly with Audrey by his side.

They'd been a proper team over the past few weeks. Not just as work colleagues but as something deeper, beyond the stolen kisses. He felt as if she saw him. The real Cooper. Flaws and all. And yet she still liked him, still stuck up for him whenever a patient began to shake their head about a prognosis or a recommended course of treatment.

Islanders could be stubborn, but so could Audrey when she believed in something. And he was hoping that something was him. He knew he had a way to go before he was perfect. Marriage material, even. But maybe she'd stay and see him through the transition.

'It's like being in a real-life snow globe, isn't it?' Audrey tipped her head up to the sky and stuck her tongue out to try and catch a snowflake.

He smiled. The last time he'd thought about a snow globe had been just after he'd kissed her. A moment's perfection he wondered if he'd ever catch again. Although it looked as if perfection could come in all shapes and forms.

'Want to get some mulled wine?'

Audrey's smooth forehead crinkled. 'Won't they need us back in the hall?'

Cooper pointed at the dozen or so people coming out of the church hall, clapping their hands and whooping at the snowfall. 'I don't think there'll be much going on there for the rest of the night.'

Her serious expression turned bright. 'In that case, I'd love some mulled wine.'

A few minutes later, warm cups of spicy red liquid in their hands, they strolled along the cobbled High Street up towards the castle ruins, where they could get a better view of everyone enjoying the midwinter evening.

Cooper pointed towards a wooden bench. 'Shall we?'

'Mmm…' Audrey said through a sip of her wine. 'Glad I wore my big winter coat today.'

They both looked at her not so immaculate white down coat.

Audrey started to giggle. 'This wasn't the most practical of choices, was it?'

'Did you buy it especially for coming up here?'

She tipped her head back and forth, as if letting the question find its own answer.

Her cheeks coloured and she stared down at the steam spiralling out of her thick paper cup. 'I know it sounds ridiculous, but after I discovered I was engaged to a cheater I wanted to feel pretty, you know? I know it's ridiculous, and that what matters most is more than skin-deep, but at the time it felt like knowing I was pretty, that it hadn't all been lies, would help. And when I put this on for just a moment I felt pretty. Caught a glimpse of the woman I thought I was beneath all the heartache. It didn't last, obviously, but…'

Cooper felt the pain in her voice pierce straight through to his own heart. He hated that she'd been made to feel so low. 'Are you still in love with him?'

She looked up, startled by the blunt question. Then, to his surprise, she snorted. 'Not even close.' She lifted the cup to her mouth again, her lips pushing forward to blow some ripples across the surface of her drink. 'I think you called it a few weeks back,' she said, staring at her drink again. 'I'm not sure I ever really was.'

He asked the obvious and most painful question. 'Why did you accept his proposal?'

Audrey sighed and looked up at the sky, awash with fat floaty snowflakes, now dappling her red knitted hat. 'I suppose I was a bit at sea… When my dad died a couple of years ago it was kind of— It was like the last link to my life as I'd known it was gone, you know? I trundled on…did my work, had my friends… but there wasn't that solid link any more. Nothing and no one to prove I'd made a mark on the world.'

She waved her mittened hand between them.

'I'm not trying to be all "woe is me" or anything. I know my nursing work helps people. But…they're not family. And in London community is a hard thing to find. Most of my friends were getting married or having babies, so their lives were extra-busy, and being the third wheel in someone else's life was never my thing. So when Rafael almost literally swept me off my feet I guess I thought I'd better jump at it. Make sure I didn't miss out on the chance to be a part of something. What I actually did was make myself blind to all the warning signs that it was the wrong man and the wrong life. Square peg. Round hole. Now I know finding the perfect fit is important. No matter how long it takes. Does any of that make sense?'

He nodded. It did make sense. What she was describing was exactly what it felt like when he'd heard Gertie had passed away. She'd been his anchor through any number of storms. The one family member he'd been able to rely on. When his parents had died he'd kept on waiting to feel like an orphan. He hadn't. But when Gertie had died, well past the age when he should've felt like an orphan…he'd felt like one.

Would slowing down, the way his gran had suggested, be the answer?

He held out his hand to Audrey and gave her mittened one a squeeze. He was enjoying getting to know Audrey. The real one. 'I understand.'

She turned to him, her eyes brimming with un-spilt tears. 'I know. That's why I told you.'

Cooper's heart began ricocheting round his ribcage like a pinball. 'Hey, don't cry.'

'Don't worry. They're happy tears.'

As she blinked, and the tears found purchase on her cheeks, he brushed them away with the backs of his fingers. She turned her cheek so that his hand was cupping her cheek, then turned it a bit more, pressing her lips to his palm. Still damp with tears, her lashes lifted and her eyes met his.

Audrey was telling him something beyond the obvious: She was over her ex because there hadn't really been anything to get over. It had taken a while, but she saw that now. She was also telling him that the feelings he'd hoped they shared were shared. And possibly worth exploring.

He did the only thing he could. He tipped his head towards hers and kissed her.

The short drive home was silent, but taut with expectation. Audrey couldn't stop running her fingertips over her lips, trying to recapture the heated magic of their spicy mulled-wine-and-snowflake-laced kiss. It had been slow and intense and, for the first time, it had made her feel complete in a way physical intimacy never had.

It wasn't like being absorbed into someone else's orbit...more like two planets gaining strength from being in a shared orbit. Scary, but exhilarating. And, more pertinently, the kiss had led to a shared look of silent complicity, and then a very brisk walk to the four-by-four to head home.

Just a few minutes from Gertie's house her heart began pounding with erratic skips and jumps. Every time she looked at Cooper—which was pretty much the entire drive home—bursts of fireworks pinged and exploded in her belly, in anticipation of more to come.

It put an entirely new spin on her feelings about Christmas and the magic of the season. It hadn't been ruined for ever, as she'd once thought. No. The magic of the season had been tiptoeing up to her in lovely Cooper-sized steps until she was ready to accept the fact that her life was her own and she was the one in charge of it.

And right now she wanted to know what it felt like to make love to Cooper MacAskill—with or without the promise of a long-term relationship.

Life was for living, right? Not for hiding away on remote Scottish islands waiting for life to find her. Which made her laugh. Life *had* found her. And much more quickly than she would've believed.

'What's so funny?'

'This,' she said. 'Us.'

'We're funny?' Cooper glanced over at her, but only quickly as the snowfall was thickening.

'Not ha-ha funny. It's more…' Audrey tapped

her fingertips on her chin, trying to find the best word. 'It's more the situation.'

'How do you mean?' Cooper asked, a soft smile playing upon that generously delicious mouth of his. 'Two lost souls finding one another in the middle of nowhere?'

'Sounds like a country song.' She laughed. Her smile slipped away, but not the warmth in her heart. 'In a way I suppose our story is like a song. I wasn't the happiest of campers a few weeks back. You met me when I was smack-dab in the middle of a pity party.'

He gave her knee a light squeeze. 'I think you deserved a bit of a pity party. What you were going through was still pretty raw then, wasn't it? And it wasn't exactly as if I was a barrel of laughs.'

'You were amazing to your patients, so I was able to see through all your gruff and bluster.'

'Oh, yeah? And what was it you saw?'

'That you're a softie. That your heart is kind and true and, while you may not always get it right, you're man enough to face the things that scare you.'

'Wow.' Cooper gave his head a big shake. 'Remind me to call you the next time I need an ego boost.'

'I mean it, Coop. You're a good man. Take the compliment.'

He tipped an imaginary hat in her direction, sending another whirl of heat swirling round her bloodstream.

'The truth is…us being forced to stay together and everything…it's made me face a lot of things I don't think I would have otherwise,' she said. 'I don't think I've ever been very good at letting anyone really *know* me.'

'You're not alone. I tend to keep my demons to myself. Not that it's worked all that brilliantly, and I know I need to change.'

'No one's perfect, Cooper. Don't put so much pressure on yourself.'

'I could say the same to you. I've seen you at work and you're one of the best nurses I've ever had the privilege of working with. And that's not just because I fancy the pants off you.'

A hot whoosh of desire swept through her as she saw the heat return to his eyes. Cooper did seem to genuinely desire her. And it wasn't one of those hot flashes of attraction. It was one of those slow-burn attractions that had started as squabbling, turned into shared respect, and now… Now it was definitely mutual.

But she owed him some more honesty before they started ripping one another's clothes off.

'The truth is, I don't think I've entirely known who I was most of my life. Daughter. Nurse. Fiancée. I attached myself to roles and tried to find myself in amongst them as I muddled along. Maybe it took having the world I thought I was living in ripped out from under me to understand what I really wanted from life.'

Cooper shot her another quick glance. 'And do you know what that is?'

It was a loaded question. One she'd set him up to ask. Dancing on the tip of her tongue was one word: *You.* But it was too soon for that. Too soon after having changed her entire life for one man to do exactly the same for another. Even if this time it felt completely different.

'I love nursing. *District* nursing. I definitely want to continue with that. I suppose I also want to prove to myself I can make it on my own, you know?'

'In what way?'

'Well, I have to find a job, for one.'

'You've got one. Everyone loves you here.'

She poked him in the arm. 'You know as well as I do there's a clock ticking on that.'

His thinned lips spoke volumes. He wanted her contract to end about as much as she did.

Unexpectedly, she saw his mouth curve into a chipper smile. 'There's always Glasgow.'

He'd mentioned that before. Was it his way of saying he wanted her close? Wanted to see if they could explore what was happening between them without a time pressure?

'What's so great about Glasgow?'

'About a million things I couldn't tell you.' He huffed a self-deprecating laugh.

'Why not?'

'Because I've always been too busy working to enjoy it.'

She saw something flash in his eyes. Something similar to what she'd begun to feel here on Bourtree. As if she'd come home.

'Is that something you'd like to do? Enjoy where you live?'

He gave the steering wheel a few taps as he considered his answer. 'It is,' he answered solidly, and then, more cheekily, as he pulled the car into the drive and turned off the ignition, he said, 'And right now I'd like to enjoy where I live with you.'

Audrey's body grew tingly as the charged sensual atmosphere that had hummed between them returned. Cooper leant across the car, cupped his hand along her jawline and gave her a deep, hungry kiss. One she returned with every fibre of her being.

'I'm falling for you, Audrey,' Cooper whispered against her lips when their languorous kisses came to an end. 'Every time I look at you I feel more alive than I have in years. Being with you, working with you, even making awful Christmas biscuits with you… It brings out the best in me, but I still worry that it isn't good enough.'

'For what?' She tipped her forehead against his.

'For offering you a future. You know… together.'

'Oh, Coop.' She took off her mittens, weaving her warm fingers through his cold ones. 'I don't think either of us knows what the future has in store for us.'

The way she said it implied that not knowing what the future held wasn't necessarily a deal-breaker.

'So…' He ran his thumb along the back of her hand. 'What are you saying, exactly?'

A saucy smile slipped onto her lips as the tip of her tongue swept the length of them. 'That maybe we should enjoy what we have right now. Who knows? Maybe we'll find out slow and steady is every bit as satisfying as fast and furious? Or maybe it'll turn out we're not a match, but we'll have had fun finding out.'

She leant in and gave him a slow, spicy, and decidedly wicked kiss. One that promised much more than a snog in a vehicle that was quickly being covered in snow.

'Should we enjoy the slow and steady us in the warm?' He nodded towards the house.

Audrey laughed, and they climbed out of the car and bundled into the house.

The second the door was closed it was as if a switch had been flicked between the pair of them. Gone was the need to talk and explain. In its place was pure, undiluted, pent-up desire.

Cooper took hold of the zip at the top of Audrey's coat, locked eyes with her and said, 'I've been waiting a long time to do this.'

And he had. More than he'd realised. Yes, he'd felt a hit of attraction when he'd first laid eyes on her, but what he felt now was deeper. He began to ease the zip down centimetre by centimetre. By the time he got to what was underneath it he knew his blood flow would be at volcano-level heat.

'You're sure?' he asked as he teased the zip past the arc and dip of her breasts.

Her breath caught as she nodded, her body organically arching towards his. 'I'm sure.'

Suddenly the whole waiting game, the teasingly slow drop of the zip, became too much. He pulled it down to the bottom of her ankle-length coat in one swift move, then stood up, slipped it off her shoulders, picked her up and carried her up the stairs to his room.

Boots, jeans and her jumper were all discarded in a matter of seconds. And when Audrey stretched out on his cranberry-coloured sheets she looked like the type of Christmas present that left very little to the imagination, but was more than enough to send surges of desire arrowing straight below his belt buckle. She had on nothing more than a lacy wisp of a brassiere and some panties. Panties which, if he wasn't mistaken, had a pattern of snowflakes dappled along them.

She got up on her knees and reached out to where he was standing beside the bed. She tugged him closer and button by button undid his shirt. Her hand skidded across his nipples, instantly rendering them taut with the anticipation of her hot mouth upon them.

She wagged her index finger. *Uh-uh,* it said. *Not yet.*

Lifting her dark brown eyes to meet his, she began to undo his belt buckle. Flames licked southward each time her fingertips touched his bare skin. When she pulled the belt out of the loops in one long, unhurried movement, he could feel the pulse of his longing press against his jeans. As she began to undo the buttons on his trousers it was all he could do to contain a moan of desire.

When her hand brushed along the length of his arousal, he found his voice. 'Now it's your turn.'

He slipped his jeans off, tucked his arm

around Audrey's waist and laid her out alongside him on the bed, so that he could feel the shared heat of their desire. She tangled her legs around his, pressing into him as she began to kiss him with a hunger he easily matched.

He pulled his fingers through her hair and gave her a deep kiss, tasting, exploring and loving—yes, loving—how being with her felt both brand-new and wonderfully familiar. As if they'd both known somewhere, deep within them, that this was the person they had always been waiting for.

Audrey's hands moved down his back to his hips, then dipped between his thighs, where the pulsing heat of his desire was building with every passing second. He took both her hands in one of his, then pulled them up and over her head.

'My turn.' He wanted to enjoy her body before he reached the point of no return. He slipped her fingers around the solid oak roundels that made up the headboard and dropped her a wink. 'No touching allowed.'

She whimpered in protest…and then again in pleasure.

Cooper could get used to this. Taking a leisurely tour of Audrey's body using his tongue and featherlight kisses to better acquaint himself. There were five freckles that formed a star at the base of her throat. They deserved some attention. And underneath the lacy strips of her bra her nipples were a beautiful dusky rose which…*mmm*…darkened when he swirled his tongue round them, teasing the soft discs to hard, erect nubs.

Her ribcage lifted and dropped in short, sharp inhalations of response and desire. They both knew she could let go of the bed railings at any time, but he was pleased to see she was enjoying the added level of eroticism as much as he was.

When he reached her hips he only had to hover above her skin, his breath barely skimming it, to produce a rippling of goosebumps. He dipped his fingers into the sweet honeyed folds between her legs, touching, teasing, taunting her until she let go of the bed, ran her nails raggedly down his back and begged him to be inside her.

The temptation proved too much for him. He wanted her, too. *Now.*

He pulled her into his arms so that their bare bodies pressed against one another. She held the length of his arousal between her legs, where the hot, wet sensation of the pleasure he'd already brought to her was almost all the invitation he needed.

He whispered something about protection.

'Please, Coop,' Audrey whispered after he'd swiftly sheathed himself. 'Now.'

He didn't need a second invitation.

In one slow, deliberate move he pressed his entire length into her. The heated, pulsing sensation of their bodies connecting was almost too much to bear.

He looked into Audrey's eyes to get a feel for what she wanted from him. He saw nothing but desire. Her hips arched up to meet his, instantly sending his body into a series of rhythmic thrusts. Her body matched the fluid moves of his, their most intimate nerve-endings set alight by the other, their movements building to a heated crescendo. Two bodies moving as one, thrusting and arching in complete synchronicity until climax came to them both.

Later, as he held her in his arms, he tried to think of a time when he'd ever felt so complete. He teased one of her pixie locks away from her eyes. 'You all right, there, darlin'?'

She smiled. 'That's the first time you've called me darling.'

'A milestone for both of us.' He dropped a kiss onto her forehead. 'Let it not be the last.'

CHAPTER EIGHT

'YOU TWO SEEM extra-chipper today.' Jimmy eyed them both warily.

Audrey hardly dared look at Cooper, because she knew her blush would be instantaneous.

Cooper carried on humming a jaunty Christmas carol.

'Is this jolly humming as you work thing because it's Christmas Eve?' Jimmy persisted. 'You're not going to show up in Christmas gear again tomorrow, are you? I claim no responsibility if you get stuck trying to make your way in down my chimney.'

Audrey laughed and shook her head in the negative. But, honestly, she'd wear a leprechaun outfit if that was all that was to hand, because she felt head to toe happy, happy, *happy*.

Making love to Cooper had opened up something in her she hadn't realised was closed. And she wasn't just talking about erogenous zones, although…*mamma mia*…those too.

Being with him had excavated a part of her heart she hadn't realised she'd been protecting so fiercely. The part that was desperately worried about pleasing other people. Towing the line. Not making a fuss. Aspiring to a love like her parents', when it was impossible to know where one of them started and the other began.

Perhaps that was why missing her mother after her death had been so complicated. Her father and mother had been one unit to her, so growing up with a grief-stricken man had been like living with half a person. A man waiting, and failing, to be made whole again.

With Cooper she felt cared for, for being exactly who she was, mistakes and all. More to the point, she knew she was in charge of her own destiny. No one else. Being intimate with him had strengthened rather than diminished her desire to pursue the life she wanted.

It was a big lesson. Particularly when she'd always thought loving someone as intensely as her parents had loved one another only came in one shape and size. But love took different forms. Some couples were glued at the hip. Some people, like her ex, used loyalty as a façade to mask selfishness. In short, every couple was different.

She was, of course, far too nervous to admit to loving Cooper. Cautious hearts and all that... But somewhere beneath the scar tissue she knew something beautiful and strong was replacing the fear and sorrow her last relationship had left in its wake.

She hoped he was feeling the same way. Maybe the whistling was a sign that he was finally embracing the love he'd shared with his grandmother and moving beyond his grief.

As if to confirm it, he did a few play-boxing moves in front of Jimmy. 'Watch yourself, Jimmy, or we'll have you in a Santa suit *toute de suite*!'

'Ach, no.' Jimmy batted Cooper away. 'I'm a behind the scenes kind of guy, remember?'

'Aye, right you are, pal.' Cooper's expression changed. 'I hear the lights are going to be out of this world for the Nativity.'

'Better!' Jimmy grinned, pulling up the leg of his trousers to above his knee.

Audrey smiled at the pair of them.

She loved how Cooper's brogue became broader and more pronounced depending upon if he was speaking to her or one of the locals. It wasn't put on. It was organic. He wanted people to understand him. He was a man who had learned to live in two worlds, flicking between the two at the drop of a coin.

Which did beg the question... Would he make tonight—the night Dr Anstruther was officially retiring—the night he decided whether or not he would stay? He seemed so at home here… but she'd never seen him in A&E. He might be equally at ease there. Or more so.

The thought made her blood run cold. Colder still when she realised she had let Cooper's presence on Bourtree, and in a shared bed, no less, influence the choices she made about her future. Exactly what she'd promised herself she would never do again.

She'd heard from Noreen this morning, when Cooper had been in the shower. Noreen had news. She and her husband would, after a short trip home, return to Australia to be with her daughter and their grandchild for good. She'd asked Audrey if she would consider staying. She'd said yes, still basking in the glow of her night with Cooper.

That glow disappeared in an instant. She was going to have to look at everything afresh. Starting now.

She forced herself to focus in on the task at hand.

Cooper had primed the needle for Jimmy's injection, and after Audrey had given the area above his knee a little swab, he gave him the insulin. The visit didn't really need the two of them, but honestly it was better with two.

Her heart clenched.

If the job was better with two, had she been

an idiot to accept it permanently? Would she spend the rest of her life like her father, feeling as if half of her had been stripped away?

Please, please let that not be the case.

Oblivious to her internal turmoil, Cooper let out a whoop. 'Jimmy? Is that you, hitting the fruit?' Cooper pointed at a bowl of apples and seasonal tangerines on the coffee table.

'Aye…' Jimmy said, the tiniest hint of colour pinking up his cheeks.

Audrey gave him a closer inspection. 'Jimmy? You've lost weight, haven't you?'

'Can you tell?' He gave his still very pronounced belly a pat. 'Down five kilos since you lot roped me into helping out with the Nativity. Cuts down on my night-time snacking,' he added with a toothy grin.

'It's clearly making you miserable, Jim,' Cooper said dryly.

'Aye, right.' There was a glint in Jimmy's eye as he continued. 'Sometimes leading a horse to water is a bit more helpful than the horse might think.'

'You mean stubborn mule, right?' Cooper gave Jimmy a play-jostle with his elbow, then packed up his kit.

Jimmy tugged on a pair of imaginary lapels. 'I'll have you know this stubborn mule's social calendar has become rather full since the good people of Bourtree realised my panache with stage lighting.'

'Oh?'

'Yes. I've been invited to have Boxing Day tea over at Angela's.'

Cooper shot Audrey a glance. If Jimmy hadn't been looking she was pretty sure there would've been a triumphant fist-punch as well.

'That's grand. Great news, Jimmy.'

Jimmy gave Cooper and Audrey a playful hooded look. 'Does this mean the two of you will stop rooting around in my rubbish bin now?'

'What?' Audrey feigned innocence while Cooper looked over his shoulder as if there might be someone else in the room who was guilty.

Jimmy waved off their feeble protests. 'I know I need to lose weight. It's for my health. And I owe you both a thank you for caring enough to mess around in my bin and get me out of the house. It's made a difference. The truth is…' His voice hitched for a minute as emotion got the better of him. 'The truth is I haven't been very honest with myself and it's high time I did just that.'

That makes two of us, thought Audrey.

'Glad to hear it, Jimmy,' Cooper said.

Audrey gave Jimmy a double thumbs-up.

She'd be here to see his progress, but she'd let him know that later. Once she'd told Cooper. 'Keep up the effort. It's obviously paying dividends.'

'Right, my friend.' Cooper rubbed his hands together. 'I'm afraid we've got to make a move—but we're looking forward to seeing the show tonight in all its splendour.'

'So you're coming?' Jimmy looked shocked.

'Aye…' Cooper answered slowly. 'Why wouldn't I?'

'Ach, nothing.' Jimmy tugged his trouser leg back into place and feigned a sudden interest in peeling a tangerine.

'No, please…' Cooper perched on the armchair across from the sofa. 'Are folk saying I won't be coming?'

Jimmy looked at Audrey, then at Cooper.

A queasy feeling churned through Audrey's gut.

'Go on, Jim. You can say anything in front of Audrey that you'd say to me privately.'

'The stakes are up at the Puffin.'

'What?'

'You know…' Jimmy squirmed. 'The bets about whether you'll stay or go. It's expanded to the Nativity. People thought you wouldn't go because of your gran, Coop,' Jimmy said awkwardly.

'And why would they think that?' Cooper asked tightly.

'You've not had a wake…you've not really talked about her to folk. And you've not said anything to Doc Anstruther. I mean, it's not down to you to make sure we have a doctor, but—'

Cooper finished the sentence for him. 'But folk are expecting it?'

'Aye, well.' Jimmy gave the back of his head a rub. 'They'd understand if you didn't want to stay, of course, but…'

'Oh, would they?' Cooper said, in a tone that suggested he was already mentally booking his journey back to Glasgow.

'Aye.' Jimmy nodded. 'Look, I'm only saying something because I want you to stay. And I've not put a bet down at the Puffin, if that's what you're thinking. What you've done for me has made a real difference. If you were to stay on… you know, as the island doc… I think people would be better off for it.'

Cooper just stared at him.

Audrey looked at her watch, desperate for this moment to end. Cooper would be leaving, and she would be staying. That was the new reality. One she'd have to come to terms with.

She waited until she knew her voice wouldn't

shake when she spoke, then, 'Cooper, we've got to get on to Rhona's.'

'Aye,' he said, his eyes not moving from Jimmy's.

'Cooper, mate… I'm sorry if I stuck my foot in it.' Jimmy pushed himself up off the sofa to see them out. 'I just… You made me look in the mirror, you know?'

Cooper lifted his chin in acknowledgement. 'I know, pal.' He gave the man's shoulder a friendly thump. 'It's something we all need to do every now and again.'

They shook hands and agreed they'd see one another at the Nativity.

When she and Cooper got in the car, the atmosphere was more like the cold out of doors than the bubbly, effervescent mood they'd initially started the day with.

'You want to talk about it?' Audrey finally asked.

Cooper gave a hard-to-read shrug. 'Let's get through the day, all right? See how we go.'

The response whipped what was left of the warm fuzzies away from her heart. This wasn't the Cooper she'd grown to know and—and love? Was that really what it was she was feeling for him? Love?

She knew she loved waking up and knowing he'd be part of her day. Even more so when she'd woken up today in his arms. She loved how his doctor-patient care went beyond the obvious. How he listened to and took on board her perspective rather than dismissing it because she was 'just' a nurse. She loved how his mouth quirked on one side of his face and then the other before his smile became complete. She loved his touch, his laugh, his scent.

But this? This cloud that appeared from... Not from nowhere. It was a troubled-childhood-shaped cloud that had taken years to accumulate. The bullying, the fighting back, the parents who hadn't been interested in being parents. All those things and more had made a man who preferred to be an island unto himself rather than part of an island community...

Ten minutes later, Audrey bundled up her frustrations and put them away. Their patients deserved their full attention right now. Especially this one. She was pleased to see the 'back off' vibes Cooper had been sending out had faded. He was, at heart, a professional.

They were about to go into Rhona Gillies's house—she was the young mum nearing the end of her journey with bone cancer—and were all too aware it would be one of their last visits.

After he tripled-checked the cooler that had Rhona's blood transfusion supplies in it, he stopped, took a deep breath, and gave Audrey a pointed look. 'You sure you're up for this?'

It tugged at her heart that he cared. Would the new Bourtree doctor care? Would he or she even notice?

She quickly shelved the thoughts. It was Rhona who mattered now.

Audrey nodded. Making these sorts of calls was never easy, but they were part of the job and she felt honoured to be a part of them.

Charlie, Rhona's husband, opened the door before they reached it. Worry and fatigue were etched into his features. It was clear he knew how bad the situation was.

'How're you doing, Charlie?' Cooper asked.

'Rhona's pretty weak today.'

'Aye, that's to be expected,' Cooper said, in a way that managed to sound reassuring. 'It's why we thought the blood transfusion would be a good idea.'

'She's desperate to see the kiddies open their gifts tomorrow. I think if the grim reaper tried to come down the chimney before Santa she'd shoo him out and say he wasn't welcome until at least after lunch.' Charlie shook his head and tried for a laugh. 'You know Rhona... Stubborn as they come.'

'Aye, well, she's proved herself a proper warrior, hasn't she?'

Charlie coughed and cleared his throat, obviously unable to answer without letting emotion get the better of him.

'Charlie?' Cooper put down the cooler in the small porch area and indicated that he should close the front door. 'We're obviously here for Rhona. We'll get this transfusion in her, which will help with her anaemia and hopefully see her through Christmas, but when I asked how you were doing I was asking after *you*.'

Audrey's heart softened. Cooper had it in him to stay if he wanted. That heart of his wasn't as hard as he thought. But he was the one who had to believe in its strength. Not her.

Charlie tugged his hand through his hair, which looked as though it hadn't seen the working end of a comb in a few days. 'I'm muddling through. Work's been ever so generous. I've had the whole month off to be here with Rhona and the kids, so I can't really complain, can I—?'

He stopped, gave his face a scrub, then dug into his pocket for a handkerchief and gave up halfway through, letting the tears fall.

'I keep talking my way through that poem— you know the one about it being better to have loved and lost?'

Cooper nodded. '"'Tis better to have loved and lost, than never to have loved at all."'

'That's the one. I used to think it was about

break-ups and moving on, but I get it now. It's about loving someone—really loving someone—and having that be enough, you know? Knowing you've felt real, genuine love even though you have to say goodbye far sooner than you imagined.'

Audrey watched Cooper closely for his reaction. If he were able to do that—concentrate on the love and the times he and his grandmother had spent together that were positive, rather than negatives—it would go a long way towards lifting the burden of guilt he felt.

Growing and learning from the mistakes they'd made was the only way to move on, she was realising. Which did make her wonder... Could she do the same with Cooper? Love him, as she knew she did, and carry on here on Bourtree without him knowing that her life was richer for having known him?

Again, she stuffed the thoughts to the back of her mind, forcing herself back to the here and now.

'Wise counsel,' Cooper said, and his voice carried a weight of emotion that went beyond what was happening in the here and now. As though Charlie's words had hit their mark.

'I don't want to say goodbye,' Charlie whispered, then threw a guilty look over his shoulder towards the lounge, where his wife was in lying in her bed.

'I know, mate. And I wish there was something I could say to make it easier for you. But I suppose you've got to keep thinking of that poem, eh? All that you've had, rather than what you haven't.'

Cooper put his hand on Charlie's shoulder and the two of them stood there for a moment in silence. The only sounds surfacing around them were Charlie and Rhona's children, laughing as they built a snowman in the back garden.

Audrey waited until the two men, similar in age, had shared the equivalent of a life-affirming bear hug. A couple of thumps on the back and more throat-clearing. As difficult as this must be for Cooper—a man who claimed to prefer to keep his patients' personal lives at arm's length—it would be a much harder moment for Charlie. It warmed her to the marrow that Cooper wasn't backing away during the poor man's time of need.

'Right, then.' Cooper finally broke the silence. 'What do you say we get this transfusion underway?'

'Sounds good, Coop.'

They gave one another a couple more claps on the back and then, with a quick look back to Audrey, Cooper got to work.

* * *

Cooper tried to hide the conflicting emotions battling it out in his chest.

Rhona looked so thin and tired. Giving her this blood transfusion would almost certainly help with her anaemia—but was prolonging this battle she'd been waging with her cancer really the best thing for her?

'I feel better already,' Rhona said, happily contradicting his silent thoughts.

Her husband let out a huge sigh of relief.

'That's brilliant news, love. That was fast!'

Charlie beamed from the end of the bed, clearly pleased to see even the tiniest peak in his wife's energy.

'How could it not be? I've got more island blood in me now.'

Audrey deftly withdrew the needle from Rhona's thin forearm and applied a cotton pressure roll and sterilised dressing atop it. 'Island blood?'

Charlie answered for her, the pride in his voice almost palpable. 'A few weeks back—late November time—Gertie organised a blood drive. It actually happened the day she passed—' He stopped mid-flow, a stricken look seizing him as he connected eyes with Cooper.

'It's okay.' Cooper nodded a few times, settling the information into place. 'Sounds just like Gran.'

'It was. It was her to a T, Coop. On the phone from her sickbed, rallying the islanders to help my Rhona… Dozens of folk came. Of course everyone wasn't able to donate, for one reason or another, and there were all different types of blood, not all of them a match. But all we really wanted was for there to be enough for Christmas—didn't we, love?'

'It's worked out perfectly,' Rhona agreed.

Charlie gave his wife's leg a loving pat.

Cooper realised it was moments like these that he'd been hiding from by working in A&E. Moments that tested the power of his own tear ducts to obey his commands. Sure, some cases in A&E had got to him. But he hadn't gone to school with any of the people he'd treated. Hadn't watched them fall in love. Hadn't shared their wedding cake with them and watched them have children, only to realise that everything they'd built would soon be shadowed in contrast to the future they would actually lead.

Did knowing all this make him a better doctor?

Cooper flicked a quick look in Audrey's direction as she tidied away the transfusion kit. She would've noticed all the things Charlie was likely doing his best to ignore. Rhona's breathing was slower and noisier than it had been over the past few weeks. Her lips were dry. Her skin was cool, despite the room being so warm that both he and Audrey had stripped down to the red and green mismatched scrubs they'd agreed to wear today.

They'd sealed the idea with a kiss, back when they'd been giggling and touching and laughing over their pancake breakfast.

Waking up holding Audrey in his arms that morning, he'd never felt more alive. But the thought felt almost traitorous, standing here, as he was, next to a woman who had, at best, only a handful of days left to live. Doubly so when, back at Jimmy's, he'd mentally packed his bags and headed back to Glasgow, where distance anaesthetised the pain of loving and losing someone.

Being here, in the thick of precisely that type of love and loss, was throwing a spanner into the works of his tried and tested escape plan. Leaving felt as though it would be the coward's route. Staying had to be the right thing. But at this precise moment he wasn't sure he could separate right from wrong.

'Cooper, are you all right?' Rhona asked, her head sinking a bit further back into her pillow.

''Course, Rhona. Just making sure we've got you as comfortable as you can be.'

'I'm fine.' Rhona feigned a dizzy look. 'The morphine's keeping everything under control.'

They both watched as Audrey and Charlie left the room under the premise of preparing some hot chocolate for the children when they came in from playing in the snow.

'Are you sure you're okay?' Rhona pressed.

He wanted to say no, but he wouldn't.

He was being an arse to Audrey—dropping a sheet of ice between them so he could sort himself out just when he should've been more open, more honest.

He'd never let himself fall in love before, and—though it scared the absolute living daylights out of him—he was pretty sure that was what was happening now. A true Christmas miracle.

'Hey…' Rhona gave Cooper's arm a weak pat. 'Chin up. Christmas is coming.'

He smiled and, as had become his habit, looked across to Audrey, who'd just come back into the room. His eyes met hers, and the look they shared was so bittersweet it was all he could do not to pull her into her arms and tell her he knew he was being an idiot.

He could feel the past yanking him in the wrong direction when he should be looking to the future—a future with her. But until he separated himself from the ghosts of his parents, telling him the only thing he brought to the world was unhappiness, he wasn't sure the feelings he had for Audrey could ever reach their full potential. Which meant he'd have to let her go.

It was a thought so painful it felt as if the ghosts of the past were reaching into his chest and literally tearing his heart out.

His ultimate decision would have to be an honest one. She deserved nothing less. Her brown eyes spoke volumes. She cared for him. Deeply. But something had shifted between the pair of them at Jimmy's, and the blame firmly fell on his shoulders.

'Coop…?' Rhona tapped his arm again.

'Yes, Rhona—sorry. I was away with the faeries there.'

Her eyes swept between the pair of them. 'Aye, right you are, Coop.'

He pulled up a chair so he could be eye to eye with Rhona. 'What can we do for you, Rhona? Just name it and we'll do it.'

She was well aware they were into the palliative stage of her care, so if there was any step she wanted to make, he would help her do it.

'I want to go to the Nativity.'

'What? At the church tonight?'

'I want to see my family up there, doing what they do best. They won't go if I don't, and the

Nativity isn't the Nativity if the whole of Bourtree isn't crowding up the church.'

He didn't hesitate. 'We'll make that happen.'

And a few hours later Cooper felt the satisfaction of a man who'd done all he could to make someone's final wish come true.

Rhona, nestled amongst a pile of his gran's quilts in a wheelchair, was front and centre in the church. Audrey had tucked hot water bottles around her to keep her cosy throughout the Nativity, and when they'd arrived Robbie's rugby team had been ready to lift the chair up and over the cobbled street, through the church's large wooden doors.

It had been an incredible moment of a community coming together for one shared purpose. To ensure a dying woman's last wishes were respected and carried out with as much love and compassion as they could muster. This, he thought, was Christmas magic. This was love. Being there when it mattered most, no matter how painful it was.

'Where's Audrey, Coop?' Robbie appeared at his side. 'Thought she'd be with you.'

Not with the way he'd been acting. Distant. Cool.

'She said she had an errand to run.'

Most likely she was checking the ferry schedule. Seeing how soon she could get off the island. He didn't blame her. He'd put the blinkers on after they'd left Rhona's. Poured all of the energy he should've been dedicating to Audrey into fulfilling Rhona's wishes when he knew damn straight he should've done both.

What the hell was stopping him from telling Audrey how he felt?

Robbie nudged him. 'Too bad the island can't have two nurses, eh? You two seem a good match.'

'Who says I'm staying?'

Robbie pulled back and stared at him. 'Seriously? You'd go back to Glasgow after all you've done here? The changes you've made in folks' lives?' Robbie shook his head. 'The island needs you, Coop.'

'The island needs a doctor,' Cooper corrected him.

A look of disappointment shadowed Robbie's features. 'You know as well as I do that Bourtree needs more than that.' And then he walked away.

Well, that told him.

Cooper found a perch at the edge of the apse, close enough to Rhona so that if she needed any help he'd be close to hand, but far enough away that she didn't feel as though he was hovering, waiting for the worst.

The vicar quietened down the excited mur-

murings of the congregation and gave thanks in advance for all those who had helped make the evening come together. Then he invited the island's children to come to the front of the church—regardless of age or faith—to sing carols and, of course, their favourite Viking battle song.

That got his attention. Back when he'd lived here, the Nativity had erred on the side of Christian tradition—Mary, Joseph, Baby Jesus and a donkey being the key players, the Wise Men, a few sheep and some Viking warriors playing a close second. His grandmother had felt the Vikings deserved a nod, seeing as many of the traditions—the Twelve days of Christmas, the Yule Log, and the seasonal ham—were theirs. He'd always enjoyed taking a role as a Viking guard back in the day. It had been his favourite because his gran had always been by his side in her own Viking costume.

Which did make him think…

'Bloody brilliant, isn't it?' Robbie materialised beside him and propped himself against the church wall as Cooper had.

The children were belting out a rendition of 'Jingle Bells' as delighted parents and grandparents clapped along. Cooper glanced at Robbie to agree, but realised he wasn't looking at the stage. He was looking at Rhona, her eyes glistening with pride, as her children went through their choreographed gestures, shaking their wrists, heavy with jingling bells on red ribbons, Charlie was by her side, his face wreathed in smiles as he looked between his wife and his children.

'It is that,' Cooper agreed, and he felt the warm spirit of Christmas slipping into his blood flow like oxygen. This was the flipside of knowing your patients well. It wasn't just the lows you experienced together—it was also the heartrendingly beautiful highs.

He let his eyes travel over the congregation, trying to see if he could find Audrey amongst them. Just a few weeks together and already he could spot her in a crowd in an instant. But her dark pixie head wasn't anywhere to be seen amongst the crowd. It wasn't the entire island's population, but it was certainly a healthy portion of it—apart, of course, from Noreen, who was still in Australia with her grandbaby.

Would she come back, he wondered, if her daughter's community was doing something similar? And if she stayed in Oz, would Audrey stay? Would the lure of Audrey on Bourtree be enough for him to finally move on from the past and make a future for himself here?

He continued to scan the crowd.

Dr Anstruther was here with his wife. Jimmy

was at the lighting console, Angela by his side, the pair of them were singing along with the children. Glenn Davidson was holding up a phone, filming two children who kept waving at him—presumably his grandchildren. All of their patients, even the poor lad who'd broken both of his legs skiing, were present and accounted for.

Where was Audrey? He was physically feeling her absence and he didn't like it.

Perhaps she'd already taken the step back that all his girlfriends inevitably did. His sour mood had driven her away exactly when she'd needed him to be strong.

Daggers of pain slashed through him as he thought of what she'd been through with her fiancé. And he'd practically done the same. He hadn't cheated. He'd never do that to any woman, let alone Audrey. But he'd turned his back on her at precisely the moment she'd made herself vulnerable to him.

The re-enactment of the Nativity began. Mary entered the centre aisle of the church on the back of a donkey with Joseph, leading her past some Vikings towards the 'stable'.

Cooper only just managed to laugh along with the rest of the congregation as they asked everyone they passed if there was any room at their inn. All of the pews were stuffed, so, no. There was no room.

He could relate. His entire life he'd convinced himself that the islanders had wanted to squeeze him out. He'd done it for them. Left with a silent vow never to return. And for what? A barely furnished flat he never saw and a sad excuse for a social life?

He could be part of something here. Part of a community.

At the altar, where the children were dressed as sheep and chickens and one alpaca, Mary, Joseph and their newborn babe were granted shelter.

Just as he'd been cared for by his gran.

A swell of music came from the church organ, eliciting a series of oohs and ahs. Two wise men and one wise woman appeared from a far door. They were flanked by Vikings—one of whom was Audrey.

A complex mix of emotions washed through him as their eyes met, an electric heat searing straight through his chest. They'd asked Audrey to be in the Nativity, but not him. Had he jumped to the wrong conclusion about the islanders wanting him to stay?

Too late he realised he'd not even bothered to disguise his dismay. Audrey looked away.

A hush came over the congregation as the

plain white church ceiling suddenly began to glow and shimmer with…the aurora borealis.

Jimmy had outdone himself. Celestial colours arced and curved across the ceiling, occasionally making contact with the handful of stained-glass windows, while the congregation as a whole began to sing 'Joy to the World'.

The beauty of it pierced Cooper to the core. He'd missed over a decade's worth of moments like these. Would moving back make him the man his grandmother had always believed him to be? A man who had the strength to endure whatever emotional storms he encountered? Or would it be a constant reminder of the fact his parents had never wanted him?

He stripped his past away from the equation and asked himself the most important question. Was making a future with Audrey or coming to terms with his past on Bourtree more important?

He looked across to Rhona. Charlie was kneeling beside her, as were her two children. Her eyes were closed, but there was a soft smile on her lips. A family's best and worst moment all wrapped up into one.

He made up his mind. He knew what he had to do.

CHAPTER NINE

'HERE.' COOPER HANDED the mug brimming with hot chocolate to Audrey. 'You'll need this after making all those snow angels.'

'I blame the children.' She pinned on a smile she knew wasn't making it all the way to her eyes. Hot chocolate before she broke things off for good with Cooper was little salve to such a deep wound. But she was determined to press on.

'I don't seem to remember it was the children kicking things off,' Cooper said, his lips trying and failing to quirk into a smile.

He'd been edgy ever since they'd met up after the Nativity. In fairness, she had, too. It could've been the journey they'd just had, taking Rhona back to her family home. She'd been understandably worn out by the outing. How much time the transfusion they'd given her would give her now was anyone's guess. Christmas Eve and Christmas Day with her children had been her wish.

Sharing a life with Cooper here on the Bourtree had been hers.

She'd felt like a genuine part of the community when they'd asked her to participate in the Nativity…right up until her eyes had connected with Cooper's. And then all that joy had been stripped away. He hadn't told her what his plans were. But what she'd seen in his eyes tonight had told her everything she needed to know.

He didn't want her to stay. His island. His complicated emotions. His guillotine cutting her out of his life.

What an absolute idiot. She'd fallen into exactly the same trap she had with Rafael. And now, yet again, a man she'd thought she loved was calling the shots.

The only thing was…she really did love this man. And the fact that he didn't share the same feelings made this Christmas Eve far worse than the one she'd imagined having back when she'd arrived on this twinkly island all lit by Christmas magic, with Cooper in the centre of it all.

After weeks of unearthing the kind, generous, community-spirited man underneath the Santa suit…the man she'd fallen in love with despite trying to keep her emotions in check… Audrey knew it had all been a horrible, over-hopeful mistake. Audrey the Optimist had been blindsided yet again.

So what to do? Grit her teeth and force herself through the next few days without saying anything until one of them boarded the ferry? Or rip off the plaster and find out what was happening beneath that stoic, manly exterior of his.

'I thought you should know I said I'd take Noreen's post, but I'm going to tell her I've changed my mind.'

Cooper's eyebrows drew together and his eyes arrowed straight to hers. 'What?'

'I probably should've spoken with you first, but...' *But what?* 'I need to start making decisions for myself, you know?'

It felt wrong. Cooper's confused expression. The churning in her gut. The weird energy pinging between them. She loved Bourtree. She loved the patients, the work, the snow angels. *Cooper.* She loved him with all her being...

But she couldn't live her life at the end of someone else's yo-yo, and if ever she'd seen a man who had yet to decide where or how he wanted to live his life it was Cooper MacAskill. As such, she needed to take herself out of this picture and put herself in a new one. One of her own making.

'Audrey? What are you talking about?'

She put her drink down and sat down heavily at the small kitchen table where, only hours earlier, they'd been feeding one another fluffy bites of pancake, laughing and sharing syrupy kisses.

'Noreen rang this morning while you were in the shower. She's planning to stay in Australia and asked if I wanted first dibs on her job. I said yes. Too quickly, as it turns out. It's clear that things between us— Well, I think I'd be better off somewhere else. I'll ring Noreen and let her know. I'll stay until they can find a replacement, so as not to have any gaps in care, but I think it's best if I leave as soon as possible.'

Cooper opened his mouth to say something. If he was going to offer some kind of placation, she didn't have it in her to hear it. Tears were percolating so close to the surface she needed to finish her piece, go to bed, wake up, and then try and get on with her life. Just as she'd planned when she'd first taken this post.

She waved her hands between them. 'Rhona and Charlie have said I can stay with them. Not as a lodger. I'll be keeping an eye on Rhona, so Charlie can get some rest.'

Cooper gave his jaw a scrub, lifted his mug, then set it down again without taking a drink. It was impossible to read his expression.

'Is that what you really want?' he asked.

No. It wasn't at all what she wanted. But she had promised herself she'd never feel as if someone else was in charge of her life again, and when she'd seen that look in his eyes back at the church…his look of shock that she'd been invited to participate in the Nativity rather than him, a 'proper' islander…it had cut her to the quick.

It had also thrown a harsh spotlight on the fact that her feelings for Cooper might easily eclipse her power to steer her own life path. The fact she'd been able to sing had been little short of a miracle. But she'd trained her eyes on Rhona, desperately trying to channel an iota of the strength that incredible woman had shown—insisting upon coming to the church, ensuring her family's life carried on as normal, because one day soon, as heartbreaking as it was, her family would have to carry on their lives without her.

'Right, then. If that's what you want, I respect it,' Cooper said. He abruptly rose from the table, poured his drink down the sink and washed his mug. 'I'd best be off to bed. It's been a long day. You sure you're all right for morning rounds?'

'Of course,' she answered quietly.

'And you're comfortable staying here tonight, with me in the house?'

Her heart squeezed tight. She hadn't meant for Cooper to think she was frightened of him, or that she hated him. Quite the opposite. She was in love with him and she was protecting her heart against the fact that it was a love he clearly didn't share.

Being part of the Nativity, a part of island life, with her rounds and even seeing the northern lights, had made her feel safer and more cared for than she had in years. Making love with Cooper had been more than the icing on the cake. It had been the whole cake. Which was why, when he'd looked at her with such shock, such…dismay, she had known she wouldn't be able to bear having it all ripped away from her.

'I'm fine, Coop. Cooper,' she corrected herself. 'Look… Don't take this personally, please. I'd stay here until the end of my contract if Rhona and Charlie didn't need me. It just seemed an easy way to…you know…wrap things up.'

'Sure.' He gave her a quick nod, with a flash of something darkening his eyes, and then, as she'd seen when they were at Jimmy's, that barrier fell into place and the distance between them widened even further still.

As heartbreaking as it was, she'd made the right decision.

'Night, then,' he said, as if they'd just decided to have porridge in the morning instead of toast. 'See you in the morning.'

And with that he turned and went to bed.

'Merry Christmas,' she whispered to the empty kitchen. 'And a Happy New Year…'

To say Cooper had slept badly was putting it mildly.

At five a.m. he put a night of tossing and turning to an end by throwing back the heavy quilt and heading to the kitchen to put on the kettle.

Why had he told Doc Anstruther he'd take the island GP job before speaking with Audrey?

Because he'd wanted it to be a surprise, that was why. Wanted to offer a future with him as his Christmas present to her.

An epically bad idea when the girl in question didn't want him as a present…or a future.

When he got downstairs Audrey was already there. Dressed in another pair of mismatched red and green scrubs, with a long-sleeved white shirt underneath, she was also wearing the elf hat from the costume he had failed to convince her to wear on the first day.

An olive branch?

'Happy Christmas…'

Her features were anxious, wary. Two things he'd never hoped to see when she was looking at him.

'Happy Christmas,' he replied, without much fanfare.

She made a tiny almost invisible wave, then let her hands fall to her sides.

A surge of frustration rose in him. Why was he acting like an arse? If he really loved her he should want her to be happy. And if not being with him and moving somewhere else made her happy then, yeah, like Charlie had said, it was better to have loved and lost, than never to have loved at all.

And, unlike Charlie, he would get the solace of knowing Audrey had chosen the life she wanted on *her* terms. He knew more than most how important that was. His grandmother had had a choice. She could've put him in care, followed her dream of travelling, but she'd stuck by him—even though he'd been a right royal pain in the posterior. She'd loved him. Through thick and thin.

Being dumped by the woman he loved on Christmas Eve definitely qualified as thin, but Cooper knew the only way he could live with himself was to take his grandmother's lead.

'How about we make ourselves a special breakfast before we head out?' he said.

Her expression softened. There. That was better. This whole heartbreak thing didn't have to include anger and bitterness.

They made a proper hearty breakfast. Cooper even unearthed one of the cookie cutters and shaped the toast into Santa and Christmas tree shapes, which made her laugh.

It was all a bit awkward…but it was *kind* awkward. A damn sight better than anything else.

She took a big gulp of her coffee, then asked, 'What did you and your grandmother used to do for Christmas? Was your sister here too?'

Cooper shook his head. 'After my parents died, she left pretty sharpish. She found herself in New Zealand and hasn't come back since.'

'Have you been out there?'

He nodded. 'Once—back when I was doing my medical training. I did a six-month stint in one of the emergency departments in Auckland, so I could meet her husband and kids.'

'Oh, that sounds good. Have you thought about going back?'

'No. Don't get me wrong, it was nice, but…' He shifted a few baked beans round his plate. 'They didn't really feel like family. My sister hated all the questions people kept asking about our past, and in the end I felt more of a hindrance than a help, so I left.'

'And that was it?'

'We sent the odd Christmas card, but the lines of communication drifted until…' He made a *pfft* noise and drew his fingers apart. That was it. They'd not properly been in touch for a few years now. Apart, of course, from his telling her about Gertie. Maybe he should reach out to her again. Ring her, even.

An idea began to form.

'Do you fancy going to the pub later today?' he asked.

Audrey gave him a sidelong look. 'Is it even open?'

'Absolutely. It's a Bourtree tradition. It opens up in the late afternoon, after most folks have had their Christmas dinner.'

'Do they serve food?'

'They do. Some folk—the elderly and a handful of singletons—can always be counted on to eat there. We're invited to Doc Anstruther's. I was going to tell you last night, but—'

She held up a hand. 'I kind of kyboshed things last night. I'm sorry for springing that on you. I just thought if I didn't tell you straight away I might change my mind.'

A tiny spark of hope hit the flint in his heart. 'Would you?'

'Change my mind?' Her expression clouded.

Cooper could've kicked himself. *Let the woman make her own choices, man!*

He rose and collected their breakfast dishes. 'Anyway, I was thinking if we went down to the pub it might be a nice time for everyone to raise a glass to my gran. You know, with everyone together and all.'

She was needed here on Bourtree. People loved her and she loved them. She'd left London seeking solace for a broken heart and had found herself embraced by an entire community.

His heart bashed against his ribcage as a lightbulb went on in his head.

She'd taken Noreen's job because she'd wanted to stay. Right up until she'd thought he didn't want her to. This was the worst possible Gift of the Magi. They were giving each other the 'gift' of ending things before they could even start.

Madness.

Especially when he knew that loving Audrey was the most important thing that had ever happened to him.

He needed to lay to rest that scared, angry little boy whose parents had been so screwed up they hadn't known what they were saying half the time. Today was the day he would become the man his grandmother had believed in. Today was the day he would embrace the future she'd hoped for for him.

One that was honest and open and courageous.

One that—Lord willing—included loving Audrey right here on Bourtree.

Today's rounds should've been enough to convince her to stay if it was just the job she wanted. They'd been given Christmas chocolates, cards, and more mince pies than any pair could handle.

Cayley had given them both enormous bear hugs and said she owed all her confidence and her future career as a costume designer to them.

Jimmy had been concocting an enormous 'healthy' trifle to take over to Angela's before heading to the pub to raise a glass to the pair of them in thanks for finally getting him 'oop and oot the hoose'.

One family had even gave them an entire Christmas pudding, with warnings to mind their teeth as they'd been sure to hide a lucky silver coin in the centre of it.

There had been some tough visits, too. Elderly couples struggling to make a cup of tea, let alone Christmas dinner. A woman with Parkinson's whom they'd found in tears because she'd stained her favourite Christmas dress after trying and failing to put some cranberry sauce in the crystal bowl her grandmother had always used.

Audrey had brightened each of their days with her smile and her warm cups of tea and, in one case, her tactical redistribution of their Christmas chocolates.

The toughest visit, of course, had been Rhona and Charlie. The couple had said they were getting on as best they could, and had tearily pointed out the small guest room where Audrey could put her things when she came over later that night. Because, yes, they had to admit, caring for Rhona was becoming harder for Charlie to do on his own.

Rhona had definitely looked less rosy-cheeked than she had the night before. But Cooper had been happy to see that once the short squall of tears had passed Rhona had had an aura of tranquillity about her. Acceptance. As if she'd come to terms with her future and made peace with her past, so that all she needed to do from here on was enjoy each and every moment she had with her family.

She knew she was loved.

That was it, wasn't it?

The one thing he hadn't told Audrey.

That she was loved. He loved her. With all his heart.

He'd let his grandmother slip from this world to the next without her knowing how very loved she was. He was damned if he was going to do it again.

'All right there, Coop?' the barman asked when he found himself, buzzing with adrenaline, at the head of the queue. 'Or should I say Doc, now that you're the one literally taking the pulse of the island?'

Cooper obliged him with a laugh, not even bothering to ask how he'd heard the news… because that was Bourtree Castle.

He was on the brink of ordering two glasses of red wine, then changed his mind. 'A bottle of champagne, please.'

'Celebrating, are we?'

'Something like that.'

'One new job or two?' the barman asked.

'Depends on how this goes,' he said, accepting the champagne bottle, nestled deep in an ice bucket.

The barman tapped the side of his nose. 'I'll lay my bets on two.'

Cooper reached out and shook the man's hand. 'Thanks, mate. I appreciate it.'

'Aye.'

Cooper nodded, his smile broadening. The plan was to toast new beginnings. Whatever they may be. With any luck he'd be buying everyone in the pub a round by the end of the night.

'Champagne?' Audrey couldn't hide her surprise. 'I thought we were going for red wine?'

'We were, but…' Cooper took his seat across from her. 'It's Christmas Day and we've both been working hard. I might not see much of you over the next few days, so I thought a wee glass of bubbly might be in order—'

'Oh, Coop,' Audrey interjected. 'About that—'

'No—please. I have something I want to say.'

He took her hands in his and, despite her vow to keep her wits about her, her brain started short-circuiting and fizzing the way it did whenever they touched, so listening was probably a good idea until she could put her own thoughts in order.

'I took the job here on Bourtree.' Cooper's voice was heavy with meaning. 'Doc Anstruther's job. Yesterday morning. Before we got to Jimmy's.'

Her heart lurched against her ribcage. 'I see.'

'I'd like to stay—but not if it makes you unhappy.'

Her skin was all prickly. Had she completely misinterpreted what had happened at Jimmy's? The look they'd shared during the Nativity? 'Go on.'

'I took the job hoping I could find a way for you to stay, but it seems you're intent on leaving. To be honest, without you here, I don't really want to stay either.'

Her heart lurched up into her throat. 'Oh, Coop...' Committing to the job here on Bourtree had been a huge act of faith on his part. Especially if he'd done so not knowing whether or not she'd stay.

His serious expression lightened. He gave her a crooked grin. 'And now I want to try and stop both of us from leaving.'

'What?'

'I love you, Audrey. It's taken me a while to strip everything down, but I've realised there's one important thing in my life and that's you. Loving you has made me whole, and I couldn't bear to see you walk away without you knowing that.'

The butterflies that had all but taken up residency in Audrey's belly took flight again.

He gave the backs of her hands a soft rub with his thumbs. 'I should've told you earlier, but I was so busy being weighed down by what I presumed people were thinking about my past I forgot to focus on what was important.'

'Which is…?' she asked in a whisper.

'The future. A future with you, if you'll have me.'

'Oh, Coop, I—'

'Please. Sorry…' He pressed on. 'I just want to be very clear. If you want to stay on Bourtree without me we can sort something out. I'll go. I'll stay. Whatever you want. I know you had choices taken away from you in your last relationship, and there is no chance I would ever do that. Your happiness is paramount to me.'

'Cooper, I—'

She tried to interject as he began to fill their champagne glasses, his words getting tangled with hers. He was pouring his heart out to her. It was adorable, and heart-rending, and not at all what she'd expected after his silence last night and his polite but distant behaviour today.

She was surprised she wasn't floating out of her chair. Her heart was so busy swelling with disbelief and relief and the type of joy she'd never imagined possible.

'Audrey Walsh...' Cooper held up his glass.

'Yes, Cooper MacAskill?' She was feeling a bit giggly now—and that was *before* she'd had so much as a sip of champagne. She wondered what would happen when she finally did have a sip.

Although...wait a minute...he wasn't going to—? Her heart froze in place.

'I want to propose a toast to the woman I love.'

Her heart gave a flip and then went all gooey. The man she loved, loved her. He was everything she'd dreamt of and more. Kind, generous, and more than those things—more than his beautiful eyes, his wayward hair, the stubbly chin she always wanted to run her fingers along.

He loved her as much as she loved him. Cooper MacAskill loved her. And it felt more real than anything she'd ever experienced.

'So…here it is. I propose a toast to you, the woman who was strong enough, courageous enough and smart enough to make me take a long, hard look at myself. I know now that I need to change. I got too blinkered. Too afraid of what people thought of me to see the people who were actually there for me. Supporting me. Including you.'

'You know I love you too, Cooper.'

He closed his eyes and smiled. When he opened them again, they glowed. 'Music to my ears, my love.' He brought her palm to his lips and kissed it. 'It took hearing you say you'd leave Bourtree to knock some proper sense into me. I know you love it here. And I do, too, all things considered. So…'

He raised his glass again.

'I'd be honoured if you would consider exploring what we have together, Audrey. The last thing I want to do is dictate how you live your life, or where, but…' He pressed his hand to his heart. 'I've finally realised mine would be unbelievably happy with you…here…if it'd make *you* happy.'

Audrey laughed and clinked her glass to Cooper's. 'Of course it would.'

Cooper whooped and punched the air. 'Are you telling me you want to stay?'

She nodded. 'After I told you I was leaving it felt so wrong.'

'Why didn't you say anything?'

She shook her head and scrunched her nose. 'I was doubting myself. When I announced I was leaving you didn't fight for me. But I hadn't fought for *you*. I chose to run away before I knew the whole story. Again. It felt like I was giving up on something that hadn't yet had a chance to begin.'

She pressed her hand to her heart, as he had.

'Knowing and loving you has made me realise I'm so much stronger than I thought I was. Seeing myself through your eyes has been amazing. So when I thought you didn't want me here...' She faltered, not wanting to relive that dark moment when she'd thought he wanted her to leave.

Cooper's expression softened into a loving gaze as he cupped her cheek in her hand. 'What do you see in my eyes?'

'Love,' she answered solidly.

'And what do you see now?' He rearranged

his features, adding a decidedly higher level of heat.

'Lust!' She giggled.

'What do you get when you combine the two?' he asked.

'The perfect combination?'

'May I propose the toast I really want to make?'

'Yes, please.' She lifted her glass to meet his again.

'To us,' he said.

'To us,' she echoed, taking a sip. 'May I propose one, too?'

'Of course.'

'To Bourtree Castle's Christmas, for reminding us what really matters.'

'Hear, hear!' Cooper drank, then grinned. 'This is now, officially, my favourite time of year.'

'Me too,' Audrey agreed. 'And I think we'll both agree that is most definitely a Christmas miracle.'

Cooper leant in for a kiss, and she was more than happy to return it.

A few moments later she realised how much the whole world had melted away when she began to hear applause and cheers, and then, pulling back, she blushed when she saw that they were for her and Cooper.

Soon enough everyone was on their feet, raising and clinking glasses, sharing in the good news that Bourtree's newest couple had sealed their love with a very public, very satisfying Christmas kiss.

Two Christmases later

'And you're sure you're happy wearing it?'

'I wouldn't want to wear anything else.' Audrey grinned, giving her costume a proud pat.

'You make an amazing Valkyrie.'

'Valkyrie bride,' Audrey reminded him primly, then gave him a little twirl. 'Cayley did a brilliant job on it, don't you think?'

'My love, you could wear a potato sack and look fabulous.' Cooper dropped a kiss onto his brand-new wife's nose and then, unable to resist, pulled her in close for a proper kiss.

'Mmm…tickly.' Audrey ran a finger along Cooper's large white beard. 'Do you think one day our children will catch Mommy kissing Santa Claus?'

'I would put money on it.' Cooper grinned, pulling his beard down under his chin to give Audrey another quick smooch before her big moment.

'Sounds as if it's quite a crowd out there,' she said.

'There always is.'

'I'm so glad your sister made it.'

'Her children are loving Bourtree. I just heard them begging Shona to let them come back every year.'

'That'd be wonderful.' Audrey clapped her hands in a happy round of applause. 'Did she seem to like the idea?'

'She did. I think, like me, she'd built up such a fear about people treating her like they did back in the day, she'd forgotten about all the good things.'

Cooper was grateful he'd followed his gut and eventually, with Audrey by his side every time he made a video call, won his sister's heart back into his life.

'You're an amazing woman, Audrey MacAskill. I couldn't have asked for a lovelier bride on a more meaningful night.'

Her smile turned into a sunbeam. 'If I didn't know better, Cooper MacAskill, I'd say you're more sentimental than I am!'

'I'm glad you didn't say cheap!' He laughed.

'Why would I say that?' Audrey gave him a weird look. 'Just because we wanted to have our wedding on Christmas Eve, and the only time was just before the Nativity...that's not a cost-saving measure. That's clever!'

He ran his knuckle along her jawline. 'That's my girl. Always looking on the bright side.'

Her expression grew serious. 'I wouldn't have married you if I didn't think we could see both sides of the coin together.'

'I know, darlin'. It was amazing, having just about the whole of Bourtree stuffed into the church to be with us as we exchanged vows. I can't believe Doc Anstruther came back from Spain!'

'I know! Another Christmas miracle,' she agreed with a grin. 'I loved having everyone being part of our day. It made it extra-special. Now!' She clapped her hands and pointed towards the doorway leading to the church. 'Go on out there. We've got to sing some joy into the world!'

He pulled her to him for a fierce, tight hug. 'You know I will always do everything in my power to make sure you're happy and safe.'

'I know, my love. That's the other reason I married you.' She popped on her Viking helmet and gave him a happy grin. 'Now, get on out there—otherwise we're both going to miss my grand entrance.'

He gave her a jaunty salute. 'Aye-aye, Cap'n. I'm looking forward to cheering the new Mrs MacAskill on her grand entrance.'

'And I'm looking forward to a long, happy future as Mrs MacAskill.'

Cooper pulled her in for another kiss, and Audrey was late for her cue. But no one cared because it was a happy day for more reasons than one.

And when they all raised their voices in unison Cooper's and Audrey's eyes met and locked, joy permeating every note and smile as they belted out the lyrics of 'Joy to the World'.

It really did feel as if heaven and nature were singing just for them on this, their special day, and for evermore.

* * * * *